P9-CRQ-369

When JFK Was My Father

When JFK Was My Father

Amy Gordon

Houghton Mifflin Company
Boston 1999

Library of Congress Cataloging-in-Publication Data

Gordon, Amy, 1949–
When JFK was my father / Amy Gordon.
p. cm.
Summary: Feeling neglected by her father in Brazil and her mother in Washington, D.C., Georgia Hughes tries to cope with life at a boarding school in Connecticut by imagining relationships with John Kennedy and Mrs. Beard, the ghost of the former headmistress of the school.
ISBN 0-395-91364-0
[1. Boarding schools—Fiction. 2. Schools—Fiction. 3. Self-perception—Fiction. 4. Parent and child—Fiction.] I. Title.
PZ7.G65Wh 1999
[Fic]—dc21 98-41580 CIP AC

Printed in the United States of America
BP 10 9 8 7 6 5 4 3 2 1

This is, of course, for Hilary

On February 19, 1963, when I was thirteen, I decided that John F. Kennedy, the president of the United States, ought to be my father.

It's not that I didn't have a father of my own, also named John—John Wintersteen Hughes (everyone called him Winter—everyone, including me, his daughter), but he was a) always working (he was a very successful banker); b) even when he wasn't working, he didn't have time for me (he was in love with Lucinda, a Brazilian woman who was not my mother); and c) he lived in Rio de Janeiro and I was about to go live with my mother in the States.

JFK always took time out from his busy day to be with me. *"Ask not what I can do for my country, but what I can do for Georgia,"* JFK liked to say, Georgia being me, of course, not the state.

The two of us spent hours going through my stamp collection. We both liked all the miniature portraits of animals and flowers and people and buildings. And Jack was someone I could talk to. Before he became my dad, I would have these running conversations with the stamps themselves. "Hello," I'd say to the lady with flowing hair on the French stamp. "Did you know that Billy in my math class is a jerk?" But now that I had Jack to keep me company, I could talk to *him* about whatever was bugging me.

JFK was a much better father than JWH because he was young, with a head of thick hair, and my father was old and balding. Also, he had two cute kids, and since I didn't have any brothers and sisters, I was happy to take on Caroline and John-John. I was Jack's first-born, of course, born long before he became president, so naturally I was the one he confided in, the one he talked to about Cuba or his back pain or how as a young man he had been afraid he would flunk out of Harvard. I could be very sympathetic because I was having trouble in school, too.

How did Jackie fit into all of this? The trouble was, I couldn't imagine Jackie as my mother. My own mother (Priscilla D. Hughes, but everyone called her La, including me) was around way too much, telling me what to do and how to do it and pressing those thin lips together whenever I wasn't doing it. I couldn't get Jackie to slip into the Mom spot, but I did keep her around in the background somewhere, maybe giving tours of the White House.

But this story really begins when my father was still my father, when my mother was still my father's wife. It begins with Christmas 1962, when I first met Tim.

Part One

1

That Christmas, my mother and father and I left Rio for a small fishing village called Búzios, which was about an hour away. It was a place where rich and important people went for their holidays, and artists, too, like the Russian painter who had a cottage at the other end of the beach from where we were staying.

Fernando, the chauffeur, drove us there in Winter's long, black limousine. When we still lived in the States—I think I was nine—we owned just an ordinary blue car. Either my father drove it or my mother did, and I would sit in the front seat and chat with one or the other of them. That was a long time ago. I never chatted with them now, especially not when I was stuck in the back of a black limo. It always made me feel as if I were going to a funeral.

It was a holiday, so Winter was in an open-necked shirt instead of a business suit. You could just see a bit of the hair on his chest and the strain on the buttons around his middle. He was wearing slacks and sandals, and I had the feeling he was wearing a costume. He kept making jokes which I didn't really get so I didn't really laugh and my mother didn't laugh at all.

Then La started talking about how terrible the American School was that I was going to. "Shouldn't we be thinking of sending Georgia away to boarding school in the States?" she asked. She wasn't really expecting an answer, she was just going around and around without going anywhere. That was how La's talking could be. Sometimes it was torture to have a mother who talked so much, but right now it meant that, even though it was, in a way, my Fate that was being discussed, I could sink back in my seat and stare out the window and become invisible. What did it matter where I went to school, anyway? It was all the same boring stuff no matter where you went.

I loved the cottage we stayed in. It reminded me of a long time ago, in the days of the blue car, when my mother and father and I had stayed all summer in a small yellow house with bright sunshine filling the kitchen in the mornings. That summer I went fishing with Winter and painted wildflowers with La.

I always carried a postage stamp–size picture of that house tucked away in my head, and I had this idea that in the cottage at Búzios, La and Winter and I could go back to being the way we were that summer — maybe part of the trouble now was that we lived in too big a house. Here it was small and comfortable and cozy, and there weren't tons of servants swarming around us all the time.

The sea here was better too, warm and gentle, almost

like a lake compared to the Rio beaches. Sometimes at home, the waves were so high and the undertow so strong I didn't want to swim. And here there weren't hordes of people baking in bikinis, only ponies nibbling the grass along the banks or, at dusk, fishermen who came to haul in their nets.

Here La wasn't saying, "I wish you would make some friends. It's not good for you to be always hanging around the house. A girl your age should have a social life." And she wasn't putting me in the car and instructing Fernando to take me to the club, where kids sat around the swimming pool talking to each other and you'd die of boredom.

As it turned out, La and Winter didn't change back to the yellow-house kind of people at all. There was another American family staying in the cottage next door, and La was ecstatic because the father was a high-ranking diplomat and the mother was very cultured and they had two daughters. "Just the sort of girls you should be making friends with," La said, with this slightly proper accent she trotted out for special moments or for people she was trying to impress.

Elizabeth was my age and Ruthie a few years older. They spent a lot of time reading fashion magazines and deciding what color toenail polish to use and what kind of cream to put on their legs after shaving. I thought about showing them my new West German stamps. I was excited about those stamps, but I was afraid they might laugh at me.

Luckily for me, Elizabeth and Ruthie had a brother who

liked stamps. The minute he saw me with my stamp book he asked to see it. His name was Tim, and he was between Ruthie and Elizabeth in age—stuck, he said, between two girls, a piece of meat between two stale pieces of bread. I got the idea he didn't like his sisters very much.

"Such an attractive-looking boy," La said, hope gleaming in her eyes. I was, after all, thirteen, and you were supposed to begin being interested in Boys, not Stamps, when you were thirteen. Well, he was kind of attractive. He was pretty tall and had dark hair and green eyes, but he had a lot of freckles—it looked as if someone had thrown them at his face and they had landed just anywhere, and that made him look a little funny, which was good, because he could be very serious.

One of the first things he said to me was, "Your parents are impossible, just like mine."

This made me stare at him. I had never really thought about how to describe my parents, and the word impossible seemed perfect, unlike La's favorite word, attractive, which never seemed perfect.

Tim spent a lot of time not talking but walking on the beach, his head down, collecting things like driftwood and pebbles. He seemed to like it when I walked with him instead of hanging out with the Fashion Queens, and actually I liked walking with my head down. I noticed things I hadn't before, like the different colors of grains of sand and the odd shapes of wood carved by the sea.

And Tim made me notice things about my own stamps

that I hadn't ever noticed before. He always looked through my stamp book slowly. He wasn't in a rush to get through it, the way La was whenever I could convince her to look at it. His favorite was the ocelot from Angola.

Sometimes he sat outside his cottage and wrote poems. Once he read one out loud to me. I liked the way it sounded, but I didn't really get it. I said, "That's good," when he finished, and that seemed to make him happy. I was glad he didn't want me to say anything else about it.

2

On Christmas Eve, Tim and I were walking on the beach together when we found a doll tangled in beach grass. Tim picked it up. It didn't have any hair, and the nose and mouth and eyes were worn away.

"Where do you think this came from?" he asked.

"I don't know," I said. Even when I had ideas, I didn't always like to say them out loud to Tim because I was afraid he'd think I wasn't as clever as he was.

"It sailed across the sea to be a Christmas present for a fisherman's daughter," he said. "And you and I are going to fix it up."

We brought the doll back to his cottage, and he painted a new face on her and cut some hair from a pony's tail and glued it on. I made a dress by ripping up one of my blouses. I stuffed the part of the blouse I didn't use under my mattress so my mother wouldn't find it.

Then Tim found a piece of driftwood that looked like a miniature tree, like one of those bonsai things the Japanese have in their gardens. "We'll make it into a Christmas tree," he said. We stole the Fashion Queens' magazines and cut circles out of the fancy dresses and hung them on the branches with thread so they looked like Christmas balls. Then we put the doll and the tree in the middle of the beach. It was beautiful—all of it. I couldn't wait for someone to find it.

On Christmas morning I ran outside even before I opened my stocking to see if the doll and the tree were still there, but they were gone. That was the best Christmas present I had ever given anyone.

I found Tim after all the presents had been opened. "Someone took our doll and the tree," I said.

"Of course," he said.

"What did you get for Christmas?" I asked him.

"A protractor," he said.

"A what?"

"Protractor. Useful for the study of mathematics. Something I loathe and am very bad at."

"Oh."

"And a shirt and a tie and a tie clip and a pair of cufflinks."

"Oh," I said again. "That's nice."

"You see, I am my father's only hope. I am the only boy, his only male heir. Therefore I must be as clever as he is and as well dressed. I was hoping, actually, for a fountain pen. What did you get?"

"Perfume. A bracelet. A dress. A blue dress."

"Is that what you wanted?

I shrugged. "I don't know," I said.

Tim gave me a look. "Don't you know what you want?"

I shrugged again. I couldn't think what to say.

Tim said, "But you see, *you* are their only hope, the only child. And if you don't know what you want, they will choose for you."

"I never thought of that," I said.

"I think of everything," he said with a big smile. I decided I would think of ways to make him smile like that more often.

On Christmas night our two families ate together. My mother and Tim's father talked a lot, not to each other but at the same time. It was a long meal. At the end of it, Ruthie and Elizabeth and Tim and I exploded out of the cottage and ran out onto the beach.

"Who wins?" Tim asked. "Your mother or my father?"

"Plum pudding," said Ruthie, "is the most disgusting, repulsive food ever invented."

"I wish there was something to do," Elizabeth whined. She sighed loudly and kicked the sand. She couldn't help it, she was a natural whiner, and besides, she had all these friends back home in Brasília, and the quiet life at the beach in Búzios was beginning to drive her crazy.

"We'll play Stalk the Enemy," said Tim. Once he told me being the only boy in his family made him bossy. "And it's no good unless everyone plays, so for five minutes you girls can forget you are too girlish to play."

"I'm not," I said.

Ruthie and Elizabeth tossed their heads. "It's better than nothing," said Ruthie.

"You pick someone to follow and you hunt the person down," he said, "and you have to be quiet."

The moon was up, so it wasn't pitch black dark, but there were a lot of clouds so you couldn't always tell what was a person and what was a bush unless the bush started to giggle. Tim and I were the true hunters, silent and deadly, moving stealthily in the night.

There were shadows and squawking birds and whirring insects and the beating of my heart as I crouched behind a bush, laughing inside because I could see Tim and he didn't know I could see him. And then he melted into a shadow. My skin prickled. Where had he gone?

In the next instant a body fell on top of me, a hand slid across my mouth. "If you make a sound, I'll kill you," a voice hissed in my ear. I struggled to turn so I could see. In the hazy light Tim looked like a ghost, but he didn't feel like a ghost, and I could smell the brandy from the plum pudding on his breath.

There were footsteps nearby, and laughing. "Shh," Tim whispered. "Don't let them find us." We lay very still, his body against mine, for what seemed like a very long time. I wanted to stay with him like this forever.

Ruthie called, "Timmy! Georgia!"

"Where are they?" Elizabeth whined. I wanted to shout and scare them, but Tim put his hand over my mouth again.

"Come on, let them play their silly game," said Ruthie. "I'm going inside."

And they were gone. Tim rolled off and jumped up. We both burst out laughing. Then he ran toward me and, whacking me on the arm, yelled, "You're it!"

For a split second I hesitated, then I lunged at him. He ducked away and I ran after him down the beach. Then he stopped suddenly and waited, stone still, as I came closer and closer. When I was almost close enough to touch him, he whirled around and ran straight into the ocean. I ran after him, screaming and laughing.

The water was warm, and in a moment Tim was diving through the waves. I followed, diving behind him, but I could never quite catch up. Just when I was thinking about quitting, he stopped and waited for me again, and this time, as I got close, he splashed me. Screaming, I slapped the water back at him as hard as I could, and we battled it out until he staggered out of the water and collapsed on the sand. I just barely managed to drag myself out of the water and fell down beside him. We sat for a moment, gasping for breath, unable to say a thing.

"Do you know who I am?" Tim asked finally. The clouds were clearing and the moon was brighter now. His green eyes were full of thoughts—I could actually see the thoughts, swimming about like little fish. "I am the Sand Prince," he said, without waiting for an answer. He picked up a flat stone and cradled it in the palm of his hand. Then he stood up and flicked it toward the water. One, two, three times it skipped across the waves.

"The Sand Prince?" I asked.

"I live all alone on a beach at the edge of the world in a castle made of sand, and I collect things and keep them in my castle. Things like shells and stones and feathers and sea glass. I write poems about them." I sat on the beach and listened. Tim seemed strange suddenly, and lonely.

"Why do you live by yourself?" I asked.

"I'm not lonely," Tim said fiercely, as if he could read my mind. He picked up another stone and tried to skip it. It plunked into the water, sinking immediately. "At the other end of the beach is the Sand Princess. She also lives in a castle made of sand, and sometimes she and I meet in the middle and we play Stalk the Enemy and we swim in the sea."

I found a flat stone, and using the same wrist motion I had seen Tim use, flicked it out across the water. "One, two!" I shouted. "Look at that! I've never skipped a rock before."

I turned to Tim, but he wasn't watching. In the moonlight, his dark hair looked sandy and his freckles were washed out so his face was white. Maybe he called himself the Sand Prince because he was made of sand. If I touched him, he would be damp and clammy and gritty, and in the morning he would be gone, washed away by the incoming tide. I shivered.

"Are you getting cold?" he asked. "Do you want to go in?"

"Yes," I said, although the air was warm and I was not cold at all.

I left Tim on the beach and walked into our cottage.

"You and Tim certainly seem to have a good time together," said Mrs. Oakes, Tim's mother. My parents and Tim's parents were sitting at the table, playing bridge. The bright lights in the room made me blink. "I am so pleased, Georgia," said La, "that you are finally becoming more sociable."

"Tim, too," said Mr. Oakes. "He spends entirely too much time alone."

"We're giving a party on New Year's," said Mrs. Oakes. "Georgia, do let Tim come and collect you. I don't believe he has ever been on a date, and he could use the practice."

"A date!" Winter exclaimed. He turned and looked at me and smiled. "Our Cinderella is going to be a princess after all." Everyone laughed. My father had a loud, horsy laugh.

I went into my room and sat on the bed. I picked up my stamp collection and turned the pages slowly. So many of the stamps were of people. Presidents, Kings, Inventors, Explorers. Had they been horrible people in real life? Had they sat around playing bridge, the most loathsome, boring game ever invented? Had they enjoyed embarrassing their thirteen-year-old daughters? I turned the pages until I came to the back of the book, which had empty pages where you were supposed to put extra stamps. I didn't have extra stamps. I would make my own. I found a pencil and drew four postage stamp–size squares, with bumpy edges the way real stamps are. In one I made a portrait of Winter with his mouth open, laughing his laugh. Then I did one of La, and one of Mr. Oakes, with his bushy eyebrows extra bushy, and finally, one of Mrs. Oakes.

At the top of the page I wrote "People I Loathe." *Loathe* is a good word, one that Tim himself had used only that morning. It is a little stuffy—maybe the kind of word my mother would use—but sometimes it expresses a certain feeling of hatred exactly.

3

For the next few days, Tim and I kept away from the cottages. There were all these snickering smiles and raised eyebrows. We roamed the beach, looking for treasures. Tim taught me how to skip rocks so they went skimming four, five, sometimes six, times across the water.

Once we had a sword fight, using sticks as swords. What would La say if she could see me, a thirteen-year-old, having a sword fight?

In the middle of the week, Mr. Oakes rented ponies for all of us, Tim's sisters, too, so we couldn't avoid seeing people anymore. We were supposed to ride down the beach. Within ten minutes, Elizabeth and Ruthie were complaining. It was too hard to ride bareback. They were used to an English seat. These ponies didn't even have bridles, just ropes around their necks.

"This is ridiculous," said Elizabeth. "I'm going to fall off and break my neck. I'm going back." She turned her pony around, and Ruthie followed her.

Tim made a rude noise, a sort of scornful spitting sound. He galloped his pony down the beach, in and out of the water. I had learned how to ride with an English seat, too, but never, never, never in my life would I ever act like Elizabeth and Ruthie. I clung to the pony's mane and followed Tim down the beach.

"Race you!" he shouted as I caught up. We galloped all the way to the end of the beach where the Russian painter lived. His wife was outside the cottage hanging clothes on a line.

"Come in," she said, as we tumbled off the ponies to rest. "Come in and have some refreshment." She had an accent that I couldn't quite place.

We tied the ponies to the clothesline post and followed the woman into the cottage. It was dark, surprisingly so, not the way I imagined a painter's house would be. She left us for a moment in the dark room and then came back in with two bottles of 7-Up.

"American drink," she said. "Soda pop." Her accent was funny, but it didn't make me smile. There was something not at all funny about the woman. She was too thin, and there were dark circles under her eyes, and she looked as if she didn't really want us in her house even though she had invited us in. "You are the American children, are you not? Me, I am Thérèse. I would like to go to America sometime. America, it is *fantastique.* Me, I am from Paris, France. A big city, no? A beautiful, big city. Here it is beach. Beach and beach and beach. Pah! It is a bore."

"But I like the beach," said Tim.

"The beach is beautiful," I said.

Thérèse stared at us for a moment, then smiled. Why? What was making her smile?

Her teeth were yellow and seemed too large for her jaw. She leaned in toward me slightly and with a leer said, "Your *namorado,* isn't it?"

I knew the Portuguese word for *boyfriend* only too well. The Brazilian ladies who came and had coffee with La were always asking me if I had one. I blushed hot. Tim seemed to turn cold. All the blood left his face and his freckles stood out.

The woman laughed. "Oh la la, it is all right, you are not too young. You are never too young."

"Come on," said Tim. He pushed me out of the cottage and flung the 7-Up bottle onto the beach.

"She'll think we're rude," I said.

"*She's* rude," he said. Without another word he untied his pony and pulled himself up on it and rode away. I was terrified that the woman would come out and find me there by myself. I put the soda bottle down and untied my pony as fast as I could. Tim was already far away, a blurry figure, not my friend anymore. He was someone I was going to be awkward with now because the horrible witch had wedged the word *namorado* between us.

I walked, hanging on to the horse's rope. I walked at the edge of the beach where the sand was wet so I could see my foot prints. I wanted to make things be okay with Tim, but I didn't have the slightest idea what to do.

I didn't see him for the rest of that day or the next. I sat outside in front of the cottages and added Thérèse to my collection of People I Loathe. I listened to Elizabeth and Ruthie, who lay on sand mats in their bathing suits not far from me. They chattered a lot as they looked through their magazines, and then Elizabeth went into her cottage and came out with a portable record player. The beach was filled with the sound of Chubby Checker singing "Let's do the twist like we did last summer."

That day went by and then it was New Year's Eve, almost time for the New Year's Eve Party. La said, "We don't have to talk you into going to this party, do we, darling? Now, you will be ready, won't you, when Tim comes for you?"

"Tim is not coming for me," I said. "He lives five feet away from us. I think I can get there by myself. If I go," I added.

"Oh, now, darling, of course you're going. There will be lots of lovely people there and seeing the New Year in is such fun."

"Time just keeps going," I said. "It doesn't start over just because a bunch of drunk grownups says it does."

"Georgia," said La, her mouth getting crinkly. "Don't be difficult. We are leaving for Rio in the morning, and furthermore, Mr. and Mrs. Oakes are expecting you."

Well, time did keep going, the day went by and the sun set, and we, my mother, my father, and I, left our cottage and walked along the beach toward Tim's cottage.

I trailed behind. Winter was in his slacks and a bright-colored Hawaiian shirt that bulged at his middle. Ugh. Someone ought to make a law saying that men over a certain age should not be allowed to dress in anything but a suit. La was wearing the same thing she always wore to parties, a black dress and a pearl necklace. Someone ought to make a law that a husband and wife should dress so they looked as if they belonged together.

I was in the beautiful new Christmas dress my mother's dressmaker had made for me. It was a sleeveless turquoise dress made out of something soft and silky. I was also wearing the new bracelet and the Christmas perfume. As I walked in my new dress along the edge of the sea—my sea, Tim's sea—I felt like a mermaid. "I am a mermaid," I said out loud. It was going to help, feeling like a mermaid. It was going to help me float through the shyness that was beginning to squeeze my stomach as I approached the cottage and the bright lights and loud music and loud voices. Feeling like a mermaid was going to help me know what to say to Tim.

And there he was — Tim — lurking in a corner of the living room, which was filled with people. He looked stiff and uncomfortable. Buttoned up. Necktie and tie pin. Cufflinks. He didn't look like a merman. I didn't know how to get to him. There were too many people between us, blocking the way.

And then I stopped feeling like a mermaid because I saw Elizabeth. Many people were coming over to me now, greeting me Brazilian style, a kiss on each cheek, but I couldn't keep my eyes off Elizabeth. She was wearing a low-cut black dress. Her hair was done up. She wasn't a dumb girl who couldn't be quiet in a game of Stalk the Enemy and couldn't even ride a pony bareback. She was a beautiful, smart girl who knew how to behave at a party.

The Russian painter was standing next to her. I had never laid eyes on him before, but I knew who he was. He was the most interesting-looking person in the room — tall, with perhaps a bit of a middle like Winter, but on him it didn't matter, because he had a shock of wild hair and bright eyes and a loud Russian accent. I edged closer because I wanted to be near them, these two beautiful, interesting people, as if something of what they had could rub off on me.

"A lovely lady should never stand alone," the Russian said to Elizabeth.

"A charming philosophy," said Elizabeth.

"And so you are — charming," said the Russian.

"Oh," said Elizabeth, laughing a throaty laugh. "How would you know?"

He laughed, too, and I could smell whiskey and tobacco. "I can tell all about people just by talking to them for a few minutes." Each word came out of his mouth like a stone—he spoke much more slowly than most people, and as he was speaking he turned, right in front of my eyes, from a dashing artist into a hundred-year-old, potbellied, not-very-good painter. How could a good painter live in a dark house?

Elizabeth was saying, "Can you really? What can you tell me about me?" when Chubby Checker was turned on full blast. People began to twist and shout, just the way Chubby Checker was telling them to. A woman pulled my arm. "Come on, ducky, dance! It's the New Year!"

Smoke, whiskey, perfume, loud music, voices, laughter, Elizabeth and the Russian—and wasn't that Thérèse, the thin wife, over in the corner? Her face looked yellow and the circles under her eyes blue.

I felt myself being tossed up by a high wave—tossed and tumbled, and in a minute I would drown. Then Tim was beside me. He took me by the hand and pulled me out of the cottage.

He didn't let go of it even when we were outside and on the beach and far enough away from the cottage so that the noise was only a thin disturbance. I glanced over my shoulder at where we had come from.

"You know what, Tim?" I said. "It looks like a smile."

"What looks like a smile?" he asked.

"The beach," I said. "The way it curves. It curves like a smile."

Tim stopped then and let go of my hand. He bent over to pick up a pebble. It was small but perfectly round and clear. "Like the moon," he said, and he gave it to me. I put it in the little pocket of the dress. "You look very pretty in that dress," he said. "Very Brazilian with your dark hair."

His compliment was a gift, like the pebble.

Then, without speaking, we held hands again and walked slowly back down the beach toward the cottage, as if all the noise were a magnet that was pulling us there in spite of ourselves. As we grew closer, we saw people clustered outside.

"Ten seconds, dears," a woman cried.

"Ten, nine, eight, seven, six, five, four, three, two, one —"

"Feliz año novo!"

Everyone began screaming.

"Feliz año novo!"

And then everyone rushed across the sand and into the sea, throwing flowers and hugging each other, kissing and crying, "Happy New Year! *Feliz Año Novo!*"

We stood at the edge of the noise and the light. It was like watching a play. Then Tim turned and looked at me. He grew very still. "Goodbye, Sand Princess," he whispered. He took a step toward me. I felt his arms around me. He kissed me. And then he was gone.

4

Fernando drove us back to Rio the next day.

I thought about writing to Tim, but I didn't know where in Brasília he lived and I didn't want to ask my parents. Instead, I sat down at my desk and opened my stamp collection to the back pages and drew the best picture I could of Tim's face, freckles and all. Underneath I wrote "A Friend."

La went back to the States because she had business to take care of there, she said, and while she was gone, Winter spent a lot of time with the Brazilian woman named Lucinda. She was very beautiful. I was left pretty much on my own to do whatever I wanted.

What I did not do was homework. It was too boring. The teachers were boring, and they didn't notice that I wasn't doing my homework. It was a big school with a lot of kids coming and going. The teachers came and went, too. Once we had five different social studies teachers in five months.

I hated the kids at school. Before Christmas I had traded stamps with a girl named Stacey. We had been friends, sort of, but then her family was transferred to Peru. Now I didn't know who to hang out with. Since meeting Tim, I wasn't interested in anyone.

So some days, on the way to school, I'd tell Fernando to stop, and I'd get out of the car and roam around the city on my own. I walked and walked all day, surrounded by the crashing, frantic traffic, the steaming heat, and the smell of rotting fruit, which littered the cracks and gutters of the streets. I went into bars and bought bubble gum and Coca-Cola. Men in white shirts leaned against the counters and stared at me. At first I hated them and their wide eyes, but then I got used to them and stared back.

I did not want to go home, because if I went home I would see Lucinda. I was afraid of her. She had dark, silky skin and a warm, musical way of speaking English. She stumbled in funny ways on English expressions. "Why do you say, *I am going out of my mind*? Your mind is smaller than you, isn't it? You should say *my mind is going out of me*." Then she would laugh her dark, silky laugh and Winter would laugh his deep, horsy laugh.

I didn't want to go home, but I was afraid to be out in the streets after dark. I always made my way back to school by three o'clock, and Fernando would be waiting for me.

At night I stayed up late and prowled around the house, inside sometimes, but mostly on the balcony outside my bedroom on the third floor. I pretended Tim and I were playing Stalk the Enemy. Sometimes I climbed down into the garden on the vines growing on the balcony. If La could only see me now. A thirteen-year-old girl swinging on vines.

In February La came home and found out about Lucinda and found out I wasn't going to school, and the next day we were on a plane flying back to our old townhouse in Washington D.C. On the flight I picked up a *Life* magazine. There was a big article on JFK. In all the pictures he was grinning warmly at me. That was the moment I decided JFK would be my father.

Part Two

1

From the moment we returned, La spent her life looking for a school for me. "It is time for you to be civilized, to make the kinds of friends who can be useful to you," she said. She wanted me to go away to a girls' school, but it wasn't easy finding one that would take me. For one thing, there weren't many schools that took eighth-graders as boarders. For another, I failed interview after interview. "You're rude, rude to them all," La despaired. "Ungainly, awkward, unkempt, no manners, and completely uneducated."

"They're all Republicans," I said, meaning the women who ran the schools and gave the interviews. "They all voted for Nixon."

"Nonsense," said La. "What are you talking about? *We're* Republicans. And I don't see what that has to do with it."

It would have been too hard to explain to my mother that my father was John F. Kennedy, a Democrat. Instead I said, "They're only interested in having me at their schools because I'm rich, and then when they meet me and I don't seem rich, they don't want me."

"Nonsense," said La again.

But this is how it was. The headmistresses stood before me with their sculpted hair and white blouses and plaid skirts, and at first they were friendly. They shook hands firmly. "How interesting it must be to live in Rio de Janeiro," they would say in their cultured voices. "Do tell us all about it."

I wanted to tell them about it. I wanted to tell them about the balcony at night, with all the intoxicating scents of flowering trees, and the dark mass of Corcovado looming behind me, the statue of Christ lit up on it, but I thought they wanted something else from me, something more intelligent, less personal, something like the blah blah economic structure of the blah blah class system, and I couldn't do it. When I tried to speak, a great boulder crushed all the words I might have spoken. I scowled and didn't get into their schools.

JFK was a great comfort at these times, the way a father should be. He tousled my hair and said, "*Never mind.*" He suggested I put all their handsome, chiseled faces on stamps and place them in my People Collection. So I did. I drew their faces in little squares on an empty page in the back of my stamp collection and called them the Headmistress Series.

By September no school had taken me. I spent the days walking by myself all over Washington while my mother was on the phone with consultants. I walked along the canal on the towpath and around Georgetown, where our house was. I memorized the displays in the windows of the Georgetown antique stores, wishing Tim could see the penknives and the glass bottles. I wondered what funny little things he would have wanted to add to his collection of things in his sand castle. I wondered if he would write poems about them.

I walked downtown to the White House and became friendly with the guards. They told me how Jack was doing, and I was too polite to tell them I already knew how he was because Jack was my father.

Then I walked home and wished I hadn't, because Dorothy was there. Dorothy had been our maid when we lived in Washington before Winter's bank asked him to head the desk in Rio. I had liked Dorothy in those days. Well, I liked her still. The problem was that before I went to Brazil and lived in a huge house with servants, I had not minded, or even noticed, really, that someone was doing things for me that I could do myself. In Brazil I suddenly realized that many, many people were doing things for me—making my bed, setting the table, washing the dishes, cleaning my clothes. Winter had told me we had to live in a big house in Brazil because of his job, and because we had to live in a big house, we had to have a lot of help. But now La and I weren't living in a big house, so why did we have to have Dorothy?

"Don't be silly," said La when I told her how I felt. "I pay her, and I pay her well." But that didn't make me feel better.

Sometimes I didn't walk. Sometimes I sat in my room and listened to Peter, Paul, & Mary. Jack liked to hear me sing. He said it soothed him, except when I sang "Where Have All the Flowers Gone," which I sang so sadly it made him cry. It made me cry, too. We'd sit on the bed and sob together. It was nice to have a father you could cry with.

Then, on October 2, a letter came from the Beard School in Connecticut. It said how pleased they had been to learn about me from Mrs. Consultant Number Eight. I, Georgia, seemed to be just the sort of girl who would thrive at Beard, and could I come on Saturday so I could have the weekend to settle in and meet the girls in my dorm before starting school on Monday.

"Aren't they even going to interview me?" I asked.

"No need," said La. "They know all about you. That's what consultants are for."

"You didn't want me to go for an interview," I said. "You were afraid I'd fail." No comment from La. "If they're going to take me without an interview, they must be desperate."

La's nose was already in the *Independent School Handbook*. "'A small girls' day and boarding school on the Connecticut River,'" she read. "Well, Georgie, that should be lovely. The Connecticut is a lovely river. 'Grades 5 to 12. Founded in 1920 by Wilma Beard in her home. Originally for farmers' children. Known for its progressive education.' Not too progressive, I hope. 'Wilma Beard died in 1960 and the school was taken over by William Bottomley III. Princeton educated.' Well, that's promising. 'Under Bottomley, Beard expanded and became'—ah, yes, this is good—'it became more traditional.' Ah, splendid, Georgie, this is the school for you. You'll sit at tables for meals and become civilized."

La was convinced that half of my problem at the American School was that there was a cafeteria instead of sit-down dinners. Private schools had what the consultants called "family-style dining."

I peered at the handbook over La's shoulder. There was a small photograph of Wilma Beard. She was different from the other headmistresses I had met. Her hair was white—that wasn't different—and her hair was short—and that wasn't different, but it was *Unkempt.* The word my mother was always using to describe me. *Unkempt* meant rough and untidy. And Wilma with the unkempt hair was grinning. There was a gleam in her eyes. But, alas, she was dead. What would William Bottomley be like? In all my school visits, I had yet to meet a headmaster. Maybe he would be like JFK.

The next day I received a list of required clothing. They weren't losing any time, this school. Maybe they were afraid we'd change our minds. There was a uniform. Blue blazer. White blouse. Plaid skirt. Blue knee socks. Tie shoes.

"Jack? Where are you, Jack?" I asked, alone in my room at the end of the day. He and I often had our best conversations at the end of the day—it was a great help in sorting things out. "You wouldn't make me go to a school where I have to look like a miniature headmistress, would you?"

"You could go back to Brazil and travel the Amazon with the man who is really supposed to be your father," said Jack.

"Sorry, Jack," I said. "Not possible."

2

On Friday night I was sitting in my room when my mother called up the stairs to me. The way La said "Georgia" sounded like soup cans ripping through the bottom of the grocery bag and falling with a thud to the floor.

"Georgia! Finish packing. I want to be ready to leave early in the morning. I would like to get to Beard by noon."

So far the only packing I had done was to throw a pile of clothes on my bed. I couldn't remember a time when I had packed for myself. For years the maids in Rio had done everything. I didn't know where to begin. Why wasn't La helping me? She wasn't helping me because she was always on the phone with her lawyer. All she did these days was run on and on to her lawyer. And smoke. She was doing a lot of that. She didn't even buy groceries. Well, not to speak of. She had bought a ton of tomato soup. *To-mah-to* soup. La pronounced it the English way. Winter pronounced it *to-may-to,* the American way. Was this why they could not love each other?

And split pea soup. Oh, and bread sticks. The only thing in the refrigerator these days was a small bowl of chopped liver pâté, cold and clammy under its little sheet of plastic. It had been there a long time. Little beads of sweat were gathering on the underside of the plastic.

Maybe after having someone else do the shopping and cooking for so long, La had forgotten how to push a supermarket cart. I thought of the refrigerator in Rio, crammed with food. It was so full of stuff you couldn't really see what was in there, but you knew you'd never be hungry in that house. Maybe someday I would have a refrigerator like that.

I sat on my bed and stared at the Beard School's list of required clothing:

Eight white blouses
Two plaid skirts
One navy blue blazer
Twelve pairs of socks
Three brassieres
Eight pairs of panties

I threw the list on the floor. I was going to hate a school that called bras "brassieres" and underpants "panties."

What about a toothbrush? Should I pack a toothbrush? What if I went to boarding school and never brushed my teeth? What if slowly, slowly my teeth rotted? Would JWH pay for the dentures? He was rich, wasn't he? But no, Jack piped up and assured me that teeth are important. *"A nice smile is your greatest asset,"* he said. I smiled a big smile at the framed photograph of him on my bureau. He was sitting at his desk in the Oval Office, and he smiled back. He would know about teeth. He certainly had a mouthful of them.

I put the photograph in my suitcase. I put in my stamp collection and the moon pebble Tim had given me. I scooped up the clothes on my bed and threw them in. Then I climbed into bed in my sweatshirt and jeans and had a long conversation with Jack about being brave in difficult situations.

3

In the morning, I came downstairs wearing the same sweatshirt and the jeans I had worn to bed. La looked at me but didn't say anything. I was surprised, having expected a scene. She simply said, "Eat some breakfast and we'll get going."

It was too early in the morning for Dorothy to be there. I felt a pang, a little one anyway, for not saying goodbye to her properly. I had never said goodbye to Agostinho and Pedro and Joachim and Fernando and Marilinda and Regina either, back home in the Rio house.

Soon we were in the car, goodbye Georgetown, goodbye

narrow streets, bumpy streets, the canal, the antique stores. Goodbye to the White House, but not to Jack, because he was in the back seat with us.

La was looking grim. She wasn't used to driving. Too many years of being flung around the streets of Rio in the back of the black car. I closed my eyes and snoozed, realizing it was pointless to talk to La as long as she was in rush-hour traffic.

But when we were on the highway and safely headed north, I opened my eyes and asked, "Will I have a roommate?"

"I'm sure you will," said La. "It will be good for you to live with someone your own age."

I turned to look at my mother's profile, her straight nose and long neck. She had a cigarette in her mouth. I wondered if I would miss her. Well, I wouldn't miss the smoke, or the cough. La suffered from asthma, and sometimes she had terrible fits of coughing. A long time ago I had believed that I could stop La from coughing if I held my breath the moment it started. Even now, when I knew how silly that was, I would try it once in a while. Probably it would be better for me to be in boarding school, where I wouldn't have to hear it.

We drove and drove and drove. First came Maryland, then Delaware, then Pennsylvania. After Brazil, everything looked neat and gentle, even the trees. The United States was a clean and neat and tidy country. The highways were smooth and pretty straight. La kept saying how lovely the countryside was, but in New Jersey she got tense again. She was afraid she'd go the wrong way and end up driving into New York City by mistake. "Next time I'll put you on a train," she said. "It just seemed as if I should be with you this first time off to boarding school."

My heart squeezed a bit at this sign of affection. I looked sideways at my mother again. It was actually better being with her than going off to this school by myself. The worst thing was that a whole month of school had already gone by. How was I going to fit in? Everyone already knew everyone else. I didn't know if I could get along with the other girls or a housemother. And I hadn't gotten very much out of school in recent years—I would probably be behind everyone else. How was I going to live with rules? Boarding schools had serious Rules, didn't they?

WELCOME TO CONNECTICUT. Lots of meadows, fields, stone walls, trees. My stomach was beginning to cramp. "Are we almost there?" I asked.

"Another forty minutes, I should think."

"I have to go to the bathroom."

La stopped at the next gas station. She reached into the back seat, picked up a shopping bag marked Lord & Taylor, and handed it to me. "Go into the bathroom and put this on. First impressions are important."

I was too nervous to argue. I went into the bathroom and pulled out the dress. It was surprisingly nice—blue, simple, with just a bit of embroidery around the neck. I took off the sweatshirt and jeans and threw them on the floor. I stepped into the dress, and then, with a sinking heart tried to reach behind me to pull up the zipper. It had been a long time, I realized, since La had actually bought me clothes. The dressmaker had made everything. The zipper stuck. I couldn't pull it up or down. I had to rip the dress to get out of it. I picked up my sweatshirt and jeans. The sweatshirt was damp, with bits of toilet paper stuck to it.

"Georgia!" La looked at me with disgust when I returned to the car.

"Too small," I said, tossing the dress at her.

"You're going to need to go on a diet," said La. "I'll speak to someone at the school. In my day, boarding schools had diet tables."

"Which you were never at," I said. My mother was so thin. Much thinner than Lucinda.

"Georgia, there must be something else you can wear."

Out came the Beard School uniform, the plaid skirt, the white blouse.

"Very nice," said La when I returned from the bathroom the second time. "At least with a uniform you never have to think about what to wear."

"O turquoise dress of silk, where art thou now?" I whispered. I pressed my head against the window as La started the car, and we began the last leg of the journey.

4

"You don't need to be so nervous, you know," JFK said suddenly from the back. He had been reading papers from a brief-case, trying to catch up with some work, but now he was ready to talk to me. *"Isn't it better to go off to boarding school than to be ignored by your mother in Washington, or by your father in Brazil?'*

I thought about it. What was I going to miss, anyway, by being at a school in Connecticut? Well, as far as Brazil was concerned, I would miss the garden. There were these huge palm trees and banana trees and flowers that always smelled wonderful. I already did miss it, although I hadn't allowed myself to think about it very much. I would miss the warm air. I wasn't at all used to cold autumn. I would miss the solarium on the second floor, where the one-hundred-year-old turtle lived. But I would not miss being served dinner every night by Agostinho in his white jack-et. I would not miss passing Pedro as he polished the brass banisters. I hoped that never again in my life would I have to feel the guilt of watching other people work for me. Besides, in that house I never had any privacy. I couldn't spread things out in my room because someone was always waiting to clean it up. Once, in the middle of the night, I had tried to sneak into the kitchen to raid the refrigerator, and a night watchman had come at me with a gun because he thought I was a robber.

I would miss the balcony. Would the Beard School have a balcony?

Was there anything about Washington I would miss? No. Only JFK. But of course he would be with me anytime I needed him.

THE BEARD SCHOOL. There was the sign. White letters on a blue background.

"Greek Revival," said La as the car wheels crunched up a gravel driveway. Before us was a large white building, with pillars in front. "Lovely," she said, getting out of the car. "Lovely view." There was a long, sloping lawn down to the river. Other white buildings dotted the landscape. They weren't as fancy as the white pillared thing—they were more like farmhouses.

"It's lovely, Georgie," La said again and gave me a small hug. "I'm so pleased for you." She really seemed to mean it. My heart squeezed again. My mother did care about me. For a moment I wanted to wail and say, "Mommy, take me home!"—but La straightened up and put on her company face as a tall man in a blue blazer and gray flannel pants came down the stairs of the large white building and drifted toward us.

"May I help you?" he inquired politely.

"Oh, yes, I am Priscilla Hughes, and this is my daughter, Georgia, who is so excited about coming to school here." La put out her hand.

"Bill Bottomley," the man said, vastly pleased, and he put out his hand. "Hello, Georgia, so delighted to have you with us." He looked into my eyes and shook my hand warmly. Well, I might like him—with a little imagination he might even have something JFKish about him. "The first thing we'll do is get you checked in here at Dolittle." With a sweeping gesture he pointed to the white pillared building. "Then we'll give you a bit of a tour, and then I know you'll want to see your digs and get settled. You will be living in Beard House, Georgia, which actually was Mrs. Beard's own house, you know, and is now the younger girls' dorm. There are eight of you in Beard now, and you will be one of the older girls, which is much nicer than starting at the bottom of the heap, and you'll be in what we call the River Room. Best room on campus, at the end of the hall, terrific view of the river. You'll feel very private there. We're a small school, and like any family we have to put up with each other's idiosyncrasies sometimes, heh heh heh." He laughed, showing a lot of pointy teeth. "Now, Georgia, you have been living in Rio de Janeiro, haven't you?" His tall frame bent toward me. I knew what was coming. "What was it like, living there?"

Well, he had already accepted me into the school, so this wasn't a test question to see what I was like. And he did look as if he really might listen. I'd give it a try. "It is very colorful—" I began, hesitating as I tried to find exactly the right words.

"Very interesting culture," said Mr. Bottomley. He straightened up and turned from me to La. "Quite a mixture of indigenous and African influences." He seemed to know much more about Brazil than I did, even though I had lived there and he hadn't.

"Oh yes," La chimed in. "My husband and I attended a Macumba ceremony one night, and the mixture of pagan and Christian symbolism was so fascinating."

They impressed each other all the way up the steps of the Dolittle Building. Girls, meanwhile, flocked by, coming and going, carrying books, chatting, laughing.

"Saturday study hall," said Mr. Bottomley proudly. Oh God, why was I wearing the uniform? All the girls were wearing jeans and sweatshirts and sweaters, and as they passed by, they would pause a moment and peer into my face, and turn to each other and say, "Who is that?" I was so obviously New.

"It's all so attractive," said La as Mr. Bottomley ushered us inside. The floor was marble; the white walls were covered with paintings of a river cluttered with old ships. Then a huge portrait of Mrs. Beard caught my eye, the same lady who had beamed out at me from the handbook.

I stepped closer to get a better look. She did have short hair, but truthfully, it wasn't unkempt so much as, well, natural. It wasn't permed or anything. And she had a wonderful, kind expression on her face. I was overwhelmed with longing. "Why can't you be running the school?" I asked the portrait silently.

"Don't worry about a thing, my dear." I felt prickles up the back of my neck. I heard a voice, an older woman's voice, slightly husky, right inside of my own head, and I knew

Mrs. Beard in the portrait was talking to me. *"You're going to have a splendid time at Beard. I'll look out for you and make sure you're all right. The main thing is to give yourself time. No one ever loves anything new right away."*

"She is splendid, isn't she?" said another voice. But this time the voice was right behind me, not in my head at all. I jumped and turned and saw a small woman with snow white hair piled up on her head. Her eyes were a brilliant blue, the blue of Brazilian butterflies. She was wearing a blue suit and a green and blue silk scarf knotted at her throat. She was as elegant as any of the women who came to Winter's cocktail parties.

"How do you do?" she asked, extending a hand. "I am Miss Pearl. Who are you?"

"Georgia Hughes," I said, shaking her hand.

"Well, Georgia Hughes!" said Miss Pearl. "You lived in Rio de Janeiro? How splendid for you! Tell me about the beaches. I have always longed to see the beaches of Rio—Copacabana and Ipanema. Such wonderful names!"

I smiled at the thought of this woman standing in her blue suit amid all the almost naked people at Copacabana.

"Well?" Miss Pearl persisted, holding her head to one side like a small bird.

I took a deep breath. "The beaches of Rio are—" I hesitated, but Miss Pearl waited quietly—"They are choked—with bodies and bikinis."

"Yes—go on." Every inch of Miss Pearl was listening.

"And there are umbrellas of all different colors," I

continued. "And boys playing soccer, and men selling straw hats and paper parrots and kites and straw mats and drinks and ice cream." The words came out in a rush, and Miss Pearl was still listening. "There are so many people, you look around and you wonder how so many people could have been born."

Miss Pearl smiled brilliantly at me said, "Well, Georgia Hughes, I look forward to having you in my English class. You must write just as you speak." With only the slightest nod at La and Mr. Bottomley, as if they were completely unimportant, she slipped away.

5

La chattered away all afternoon, laughing with Mr. Bottomley and with the housemothers, Miss Hagman and Mrs. Gross, and with any girls who happened to pass by. It almost seemed as if she were the one who was coming to the school. She gushed about everything — the classrooms, the hockey fields, the dining room, the auditorium where morning meeting and assemblies were held, and then Beard House, where I would be living.

Beard had been a real house once, unlike Grady, the ugly new dormitory for the older girls. That dorm looked like a factory building, all cinder block, with the girls' rooms all exactly alike lined up along straight hallways. Beard House was an old two story farmhouse, with living rooms, a dining room and a kitchen on the first floor, and girls' rooms and bathrooms on the second. My room was at the end of a long, dark hallway.

The best thing about this room, as far as I was concerned, was the view of the river. There it was at the bottom of the sloping lawn, sparkling under a blue October sky. I stood and stared at it. I hadn't expected a river to be part of boarding school. It seemed like a wild, beautiful, free thing.

"It's dear and quaint, Georgie," La said, looking around at the chintz curtains and the fresh white walls. About the girl who was going to be my roommate, Sidney Callahan, she said, "What an attractive girl."

At first sight, I did not like Sidney Callahan. She was too tall, her hair was too blond, her ponytail was too perky (one of Tim's words), and she had a loud, brash voice.

"So lucky," said La. Then she turned to me and with a smoky peck on my cheek said, "I must be going, darling, it's a long drive. I know they will take very good care of you here."

And she was gone. Suddenly I was alone with Sidney Callahan, who had been kept from going to a movie with the other Beard House girls so that she could meet her new roommate.

"My best friend, Amy Glass, was rooming with me until you came," was the first thing Sidney said to me as she sat on her bed and watched me unpack. "They decided to split us up, so Amy's downstairs now with Harriet Hickson. Poor Amy!"

I sat down on my bed. "I don't have to—"

"You do have to," she said. "And so does Amy. It was Miss Pearl's idea. And now Amy has to live with Harriet, who's from this little fishing village in Nova Scotia. Her father is a fisherman. You have to wonder what she's doing here. I mean, God, she's literally a fish out of water, and she's so homesick, just literally crying all the time. Her mother went to Beard, so she sent Hatty, but my daddy says that's not a good reason to send your kid away to a school. He's a trustee, so he should know. By the way, I hear your father is as rich as mine."

Where had she heard that? I thought of Mr. Bottomley, with his shark's smile and his fleshy handshake and the fact that I'd been accepted to the school without anyone meeting me.

"Actually, my father is dead," I said. I opened my suitcase and took out the picture of JFK.

Sidney looked startled. "Oh, I'm sorry—I didn't know—I thought—"

"It's okay," I said. "It's recent. Not many people know about it yet. It's why I'm here. My mother—she's having a real hard time."

Sidney stared. "Geez, I never would have guessed—she seemed so—"

"Perky," I said.

There was a picture hook on the wall beside my bed. I

carefully hung JFK on it. There. He could look down at me at night.

"Are you really going to keep that picture up there?" Sidney asked. "My Daddy can't stand him."

"It—the picture belonged to my father," I said. "It's all I have left of him."

"Gee, I'm sorry," said Sidney. She seemed speechless for a moment, but then she said, "Is that all you're going to put up?" she asked.

"That's all I have," I said.

Sidney's side of the room was covered with football pennants and large photographs of football players in their helmets and uniforms, with messages scrawled in large black letters across their bodies. "To Sid, a real cute girl. Love, Billy." "To Sid, Watch out! I'll be waitin' for ya! Love, Dougie."

There was a racket suddenly of girls' voices and footsteps racing down the hall into the River Room. "Here they come," said Sid. "Get ready."

A small girl with black hair cut into straight bangs across her forehead burst into the room. Sparks seemed to fly out of her. "Hi, I'm Lulu LaBombard, pleased to meetcha. I'm in the sixth grade. Can you believe it? I bet you thought I was older. Hey, you come from Brazil, you must be a Brazil nut, that's so cool. Do you speak Spanish? I know Spanish."

"Portuguese," I said automatically. I was used to people thinking I knew Spanish. Even some of the headmistresses who had interviewed me thought Spanish was the language spoken in Brazil.

"Hey, the best gangs in Brooklyn are Spanish," Lulu said, as if she hadn't heard. "Gabriela in our dorm is Spanish, you can talk to her—hey, you think gangs are bad? Don't say nothing about them, okay, unless you know what you're talkin' about, okay, like stereotyping people ain't good, you know what I mean? I mean, my mother says I gotta come here because I hang out too much with those kids, but what does she know about them? Hey, I bet the Brazilian guys are cute. I knew a Brazilian guy once, cutest guy, cutest accent, cutest rear end I ever saw."

Behind Lulu was another girl, who said, "Hi, I'm Harriet, but you can call me Hatty." Overall, there was something pale and, well, wet about her. She had scraggly pale red hair and a very pimply forehead, and her pale blue eyes oozed water. She fluttered around my bed like a soggy moth. "Can I do anything to help you, unpack or anything?" she asked in a pale, wet voice. I had to admit I could see why Sid didn't like her that much.

Then two other girls rushed in and bounced toward me. They looked so young I couldn't believe they were in boarding school. They had long hair that they wore in identical pigtails. "Abby," said one, and "Addy," said the other. "Hi ya, are you really from Brazil?" said one, and, "See ya later, gotta hurry before the supper bell!" said the other one. "Let me wear your sweater tonight, Abs, okay, the blue one?" Addy yelled as they ran down the hall.

Then a girl with long black hair and very white skin came just to the door frame and poked her head in. "Nice to meet you," she said to me very slowly and formally and with a bit of an accent. "Come talk to me about Brazil sometime. I live far away, too, in Spain." She turned around and disappeared before I could say anything.

They had all come in so fast I wasn't sure I could keep them straight. Then a tall, skinny girl with a long neck and squinty eyes walked in slowly and sat coolly and quietly on Sid's bed. Was this Amy Glass? She finally opened her mouth to speak. "I don't see why you couldn't live with someone else and I could stay here with Sid," she said. Hatty and Lulu were sitting on my bed right next to me, and I could feel them both shrivel a bit as Amy spoke.

"Well, maybe I could," I said. "I don't have to be here."

"You have to," said Amy, squinting her squinty eyes. "It was Miss Pearl's idea to separate us, and what she says goes. Don't let anyone kid you that Mr. Bottomley runs this school. It's really that old witch."

Then from downstairs came the clanging of a bell. "Supper bell," said Sid. "Come on, free seating, let's get a good seat." She and Amy jumped up and ran down the stairs. Lulu grabbed my hand and said, "Come on, Brazil Nut, you gotta eat to live, ya know," and she pulled me downstairs, with Hatty following close behind.

I allowed Lulu and Hatty to tow me to the Dolittle dining room. "It's Saturday night," Lulu said. "We eat buffet style and we can sit anywhere we like."

There were so many girls, most of them older, and there was so much noise, and it was all so unfamiliar, I felt as if I were in a very strange dream.

A man with a bristling mustache stood up and rang a bell and said, "Keep your voices down." There were a few seconds of almost scary silence until someone laughed (I think it was Sid), and then the voices started up and pretty soon everyone was shouting again. The man with the mustache rang his bell again.

"It would be extremely pleasant to be able to speak to one's dinner companions without having to raise one's voice," he said. "We are in a school for young ladies, not at a cattle market." Loud fake laughter. Sid? "As my hearing is in danger of being permanently affected by the decibel level, we will now have two minutes of complete silence."

"That's Mr. Tweed," Lulu whispered to me. "He's in charge of the boarding department."

After what I guess was two minutes, Mr. Tweed stood up and said, "You may now speak again in the dulcet tones of civilized young ladies."

Lulu stuffed a brownie into her mouth and said, "Mooo," and bits of chocolate went flying out of her mouth. This was supposed to be better than the cafeteria at the American School?

After the meal, Lulu dragged me back to Beard House, and Miss Hagman went through the rules of the school and the dorm routines with me while the other girls watched TV. I nodded my head a lot while she droned on, but I was sure I would never keep it all straight—what time to get up, when to take a shower, when to turn the lights out. I had the worst headache I had ever had in my life. The other girls were still watching the Saturday night movie. All I wanted to do was be by myself, so I crept upstairs hoping no one would see me, because I had a feeling it was weird to want to be by myself.

My room was amazingly peaceful without anyone in it. I got out my stamp collection, sat on my bed, and leafed through the pages. When I came to the ocelot from Angola, I stopped. I could almost see Tim's hair flopping into his eyes as he looked at the stamp. I could almost taste the warm sea air of Búzios. If I kept looking at the book, maybe I could go back to that time. Maybe I wouldn't have to be here at boarding school at all.

Amy and Sid clattered into the room. I didn't have time to shut the book before Amy zeroed in on it. "Stamps," she sniffed in disbelief. "You collect stamps? Aren't you a little old for that?" She turned her back and put a record on Sid's record player. It was Frank Sinatra singing "Once in Love with Amy." Amy and Sid sang along, screaming the words at the top of their lungs. I sat on my bed watching them. Was I invisible or what? How come they didn't talk to me at all?

My head hurt so much. I put on my pajamas and crawled into bed.

"Oops," said Sid, suddenly noticing me. "Maybe we better go somewhere else. Didn't mean to keep you up."

Amy and Sid ran giggling from the room. I went over to the window and looked out. In the dark night, the lights of the other school buildings blazed. Beyond them was the river. It was strange to think of that huge piece of water out there with boats on it and fish in it and maybe ducks curled up sleeping along its edges, if ducks hung around in the fall — I wasn't really sure. Somehow the thought of the river made me feel better.

It wasn't long before the quiet hour bell rang. It was called quiet hour even though it was only half an hour. Sid came in. I realized that without Amy around, Sid was much nicer. She asked me what I thought of the other kids in the dorm. I didn't know what to say, so I asked, "How old are Abby and Addy? They seem so young."

"Fifth grade," she said.

"Fifth grade? Yikes!"

"Beard is one of the few schools that takes kids so young," she said. "That's one of its claims to fame. Sometimes there are actually tons of younger boarders, like when I first came here two years ago, but every year there have been fewer kids. Daddy says Mr. Bottomley might be on his way out because he isn't filling the beds. Daddy's a trustee so he knows all the dirt."

I thought again of how the school had accepted me sight unseen. "Daddy says the school isn't changing enough with the times, and that's why they're having trouble keeping kids here," she said. "I mean, the Hag — Mrs. Hagman — is a hundred years old, she's never been married or had kids or anything, and she treats us the same way girls were treated a hundred years ago."

I sat listening with a sinking heart. Why had La sent

me to this school? "Why do you go here?" I couldn't help asking her. "I mean, if your father thinks, and you think, it's not that great?"

"It's just that I'm used to it now—I have friends and everything. It would be hard to change." She tossed her head. "And my grades aren't that great. I'd have to get better grades."

"Couldn't you go to public school at home?"

Sid laughed her loud, brash laugh. "Daddy would never let me go to a public school."

I looked away. There was something about Sid that embarrassed me. Maybe it was the way she always called her father "Daddy." Maybe I was jealous or maybe she was making me realize it was weird that I called my father Winter.

"And get a load of the housemothers," said Sid. "The Hag is really the Boss, you know. Mrs. Gross is just here so the Hag can have a day off now and then. The Hag was born to be a housemother, but I think Grossie was an actress or something once upon a time, and then when her husband died, she went crazy."

Come to think of it, Mrs. Gross did look odd. She had a lot of messy hair piled up on her head, very plucked eyebrows, round blotches of rouge on her cheeks, and bright red lipstick. She seemed sort of nice, though—at least she smiled a lot, unlike Miss Hagman of the iron gray hair and the sixty-foot-wide bosom. Miss Hagman hadn't even smiled much at La.

"Grossie literally belongs in a nut house," Sid continued,

"but because she's not violent or anything, she got a job here instead. Oh," she said looking at her watch. "It's lights out. If we don't go to bed now, the Hag'll come up and nag and think of some terrible torture."

We turned out our lights and Sid told me more about her father. He had something to do with the National Football League, and he was talking to Gabriela's father about buying a castle in Spain so they could go there for vacations, and then she told me about her mother, who was from some important rich New York family, and then she told me about her wonderful, adorable brother, Ross, who went to St. Andrew's, the boys' school across the river from Beard, and by the time she got to her wonderful, adorable Weimeraners, which after a while I figured out were dogs, I was pretty much asleep. I figured JFK wouldn't mind listening to whatever other wonderful, adorable things the Callahan family was up to.

• • •

In the new notebook Mr. Tweed had given me for school, I wrote:

> *Dear Jack,*
> *It is Sunday night. We went to church this morning. We have to go to church. I didn't know which one to choose because La and Winter never go, at least they haven't since we lived in Brazil. La used to take me when I was little, but I don't know what church we went to except it was huge and I thought the people in the*

stained glass windows were angels. I finally decided to go with Lulu to the Catholic church because she wanted me to and because you're Catholic, aren't you, Jack? I thought you would like that. But I didn't know when to kneel and when not to, and Lulu had to keep yanking me up and down. We had to wear stockings and white gloves and a hat. I actually didn't mind. It was sort of a relief to be dressed up and to wear nice shoes instead of those cloddy ones I'm going to have to wear to school. But La sent me here with only a few skirts and one dress. Sid has about a hundred, which she leaves all over the room. She is a slob. She also has nice pillows with flowery pillowcases. My pillow is the school one—it's flat and clumpy and covered with this scratchy grayish white pillowcase. Oh well.

Lulu is funny and talks a lot about her friends back home in Brooklyn, and Hatty talks a lot about her family in Nova Scotia. Abby and Addy always stick together, and Gabriela never comes out of her room. Amy is always in this room, and whenever she's here, Sid ignores me. Right now they're sitting on Sid's bed laughing and talking about who has the best hair in school. They say Allison Clarke, who is a junior. Darn. I thought it was me.

Tomorrow we have classes. I don't know how that's going to be.

From me, your wonderful,
smart, loyal, and brave daughter,
Georgia

6

My first day.

7:15: First bell. Sid rolled over and groaned.

7:20: Kicked off my blankets and stood up on the cold floor. Sid pulled the covers over her head.

7:30: Got dressed. Panties. Brassiere. White blouse, plaid skirt, blue knee socks, tie shoes. Sid stayed in bed.

7:32: Brushed my hair while staring out the window. The other buildings, the hockey fields, the river, were hidden in a gray mist. Made my bed. Sid poked her head out of the covers. "Why are you making your bed?" she asked. "Gertie, the maid, is supposed to do that." I shrugged. I wasn't going to tell Sid that in my new life, servants were not going to do things I could do for myself.

7:45: Second bell.Time to leave Beard House and walk up to Dolittle for breakfast. Sid finally out of bed. I put on the Beard School blue blazer. It had an emblem on the pocket, a sort of badge with a B on it. It made me feel like a soldier going to war. I opened my top drawer—I had to yank it to get it open—talk about the crummy furniture at this school!—and took out the moon pebble and put it into my blazer pocket. Maybe it would help me get through the day. I went downstairs to look for Lulu because I wasn't sure I wanted to go to breakfast by myself, but Lulu was still in the shower, and actually I decided I liked being on my own.

As I was going out the door, a maid was coming in. She

was wearing a white blouse and a black skirt. "Hi, you must be the new one," she said. "How do you do?" I shook her hand and said, "I'm Georgia Hughes." The maid laughed. "Nice manners," she said. "That's a breath of fresh air. I'm Gertie, and you let me know, Georgia, if you ever need anything."

8:00: Breakfast. We had to stand behind our chairs and wait for all the boarding students to get there. I was slightly out of breath because it was a bit of a walk uphill to get to Dolittle. Sid was late. Lulu was late. Hatty was late. Mr. Tweed lectured the dining room on the importance of Being Prompt. Lucky me. I got to sit at his table. He sat at one end. Mrs. Tweed sat at the other.

The entire room ate silently during breakfast. I figured Mr. Tweed would like this, but he leaned forward suddenly and pointed to the girl sitting across from me. "Take your elbows off the table, Hilary," he said. And to the girl next to me, "Drink your orange juice, Laurie." Lulu, on my other side, poked me in the side with her elbow. She dumped a ton of sugar on her cereal.

"Don't put so much sugar on your cereal, Lulu," said Mr. Tweed. Lulu poked me again and I poked her back. Family-style dining was the greatest.

8:30: Morning Meeting. This was in the auditorium, which was really a big gym with a stage at one end of it. The students sat in rows, by classes, youngest in front. As I came in with Lulu, I spotted Abby and Addy. I was trying hard to learn how to tell them apart. I thought Addy had the sharp nose and Abby the eyebrows that almost came together in the middle. Lulu showed me where I was supposed to sit. Behind me were the older girls. Some even leaned forward and asked me what it was like to live in Brazil. How did they know I lived in Brazil? I said, "I don't live there anymore. I live in Washington, D.C." They said, "Oh." I felt as if I wasn't very good at this conversation stuff, because no one seemed to know what to say to me next. Oh well. It was time for the morning thing to begin anyway. Mr. Bottomley stood up in front of us, with all the teachers behind him, and led the school in the opening hymn. "Almighty Father, strong to save, whose arm hath bound the restless waves." Well, here I was in a sea, all right, a sea of blue blazers—was I going to perish in the restless waves? Almighty Father—was that JFK?—could he save me?

8:45: First period. Miss Payne for math. Pre-algebra. I couldn't remember ever having anything like this before, but I might have—that last year at the American School was pretty hazy. Miss Payne moved fast and didn't seem like the most patient person in the world. I suspected this class was not going to go well for me.

9:30: Second period. History. Mr. Tweed. He lectured about the Industrial Revolution. The class was busy taking notes. I took about half a page of notes in my new notebook, the one I used to write a letter to JFK, and then I lost the thread of what he was saying as I began to study his mustache. Why didn't he trim it? I was afraid this class was not going to go well for me.

10:15: Third period. English. Miss Pearl. She asked the class to write a paragraph describing our favorite place. “Use your senses—make me feel the place.” I thought about the balcony in Rio. Oh, no—was I actually homesick? I wrote a few sentences, hoping that no one could see I was trying not to cry. I didn't like what I had written, so I started over. Finally I was finished.

> *I like the balcony of my house in Rio. I especially like to walk there at night. The air is filled with the sweet smell of jacaranda, which drips red blossoms into my hands. Beneath my bare feet, I can feel the tiles, warm and sweating. When I walk there at night, I play a game of looking backward over my shoulder at the lighted statue of Christ, which stands on the Corcovado, the rock mountain behind my house. If I look backward quickly, the statue seems to be suspended in air because Corcovado is invisible in the darkness. Also in the darkness are the favelas, the shacks on the hillside where the poor people live, and their music floats down to me in the sweet-smelling air.*

Miss Pearl asked the class to read aloud. When it was my turn, my voice shook. I had never read out loud anything I had written before. Actually, I had never written about something I cared about before. My entire body was shaking. “Well, Miss Hughes!” Miss Pearl exclaimed when I finished. I was not sure if that meant that what I had written was good or bad, but the other girls in the class looked at me with interest. Maybe *this* class was going to go well.

11:00: Recess. Recess seemed to be the time when you could pick up your mail. Clusters of laughing and chattering girls gathered around the mailboxes. Hatty appeared with her watery eyes and asked how I liked school. I knew I should have been grateful for Hatty's friendliness, but somehow it felt like a heavy weight. There were no letters waiting for me in my mailbox.

11:15: Fourth period. Art. Miss Fern. Every time Miss Fern started to say something, all the girls talked and interrupted her. Finally Miss Fern said, "Today you may have free drawing. And I want to see something by the end of the period. If you are going to be disruptive, I will have to send you out." Hatty sat next to me. Sid was in the class, too. She plunked herself on the other side of the studio with most of the other girls, and they sat and talked to each other. Now and then Miss Fern came over and told them to get to work. I liked to draw—in fact, art was the one class at the American School I had liked. I wanted to draw the beach at Búzios, but I needed to concentrate to remember it right. I wished Miss Fern could get the girls to be quiet. Miss Fern looked about fifteen, and there was something funny about her eyes—she had a fuzzy look, as if she couldn't see properly. Maybe that was why no one listened to her. I drew the beach, with a piece of driftwood in the foreground. And then I tried to sketch Tim standing in the waves.

Sid came over and looked at the drawing and asked, "Is that your boyfriend?" Other girls came over and started asking me questions about Brazil, and I wished they would leave me alone, and then Miss Fern told them all to sit down and be quiet.

12:00: Fifth period. Science. Miss Pitt. Miss Pitt was young and popular with the girls. She laughed a lot and called everyone by their last names. I didn't like being called by my last name, and I thought Miss Pitt laughed too much. I understood about half of what she talked about (tectonic plates). This class was not going to go well.

12:45: Lunch. I was assigned to Miss Fern's table. I looked around for Lulu, but then I realized there was no one younger than eighth grade in the dining room. I sat next to Miss Fern who was struggling to serve soup. Poor Miss Fern, nothing seemed to be easy for her. All the girls at the table had been at this school forever. They said things like, "Remember in ninth grade when Hilary got sick in Latin class?" and then they laughed really hard. They made ninth grade seem like a hundred years ago, as if they had been babies back then. Would I ever feel that way? Would I still be at Beard when I was sixteen, seventeen? I couldn't imagine being at Beard that long. I could hardly imagine being there another day.

1:00: Sixth period. French. Madame Lefèvre. Her hair was dyed and she wore a lot of makeup and jewelry and perfume and a shiny dress and high-heeled shoes. Compared to the other teachers at Beard (except for Miss Pearl, of course), with their no-nonsense hairdos and white blouses and cardigan sweaters and wool skirts and sensible shoes, Madame looked as if she came from a different planet. She smelled like Rio. I felt a wave of homesickness. I didn't think I belonged in a no-nonsense school where only the French teacher wore perfume. The class was on the third chapter of the textbook, but French was so much like Portuguese I thought it would be easy.

1:45: Afternoon study hall. The girls sat in a large room, the desks in rows. A senior girl came over and explained the study hall rules to me. There were lots of them — how to ask to go to the bathroom and so on. Miss Fern was running the study hall, or at least she sat in front of the room, but in spite of all the rules, everyone talked and passed notes. I didn't have anyone to pass notes to. I could do homework (there seemed to be a ton of it), but it had been so long since I had done homework, the very thought of it made me want to go to sleep.

2:30: Sports. Field hockey with Miss Pitt and Miss Fern. Miss Pitt took the good players like Sid and Amy. Miss Fern took everyone else. She didn't seem to know very much about field hockey. Some of the girls snuck off behind the goal and hid in the trees, and Miss Fern never realized they were missing. I stood on the side and watched the other girls hit balls back and forth to each other. Hatty came over and said, "Come on, I'll show you how to hold the stick." But we couldn't find a stick for me, so I ended up sitting down and doing nothing, which I wouldn't have minded except that it was cold sitting on the ground.

4:30: Sports was over. Time to go back to the dorm. We were supposed to shower and change for supper. We were supposed to wear a skirt or a dress to supper. I had only two skirts that weren't uniform skirts. Big choice—the plaid one or the navy blue one? Sidney spent a lot of time before supper trying different things on.

6:00: Supper. Back at the Tweeds' table. Lulu sat next to me and chattered about her day. It was actually a relief to have someone to talk to.

6:45: Evening study hall. This time Mr. Tweed ran it. This time it was quiet. No one talked at all. Each girl was looking intently at a book or writing earnestly in a notebook. I opened my math book and stared at it for a moment and then decided that this was not for me.

My eyes wandered from the book to the rows of girls. Most of them had long hair, which they wore in ponytails or braids or pigtails. They wore plaid skirts or pleated navy blue skirts or frilly dresses or plain ones with pearl necklaces around their necks and pearl earrings in their ears. Some of the girls were wearing knee socks, some stockings. Almost everyone was wearing loafers, but a few had on flats. Although they all looked slightly different from each other, they all looked as if they belonged at Beard. Not me, though. I knew I didn't and I knew I never would.

I put the math book down and opened the French book. It was new and stiff and I had to hold it with both hands to keep it open.

I thought about Tim. I put down the French book and opened the stamp collection, which I had been carrying around all day. I turned to the back of it and stared at my picture of Tim. Did it really look like him? Where was he now? How was he now? What was he doing right this minute?

It was so strange to think there was another world out there, outside of study hall. Somewhere there were families who actually lived in houses that had refrigerators full of food, and their kids were sitting at the dining room table doing homework.

I glanced over at a girl who was sleeping behind her propped-open books. Long dark hair covered her face. Good idea, maybe I could try it. But just then Mr. Tweed rose from his desk and marched down the aisle and rapped the girl sharply on the shoulder. "This is not a bedroom," he whispered loudly. The girl sat up and rubbed her eyes.

I decided to talk to my father.

"Listen, Jack, I don't want to be here."

"I know, but we need you here. I couldn't tell you this before, but now you're ready to know. The Beard School is a cover, it's not really a school."

"It's not?"

"No, it's a cover for a gunrunning operation to Cuba."

"It is?"

"Every night boats come up the Connecticut and stop at the old boathouse down there. They pick up guns and transport them to Cuba. That's how Fidel is staying in power."

"But who's supplying the guns?"

"Bottomley, Tweed, and Payne. It's a conspiracy, and they are at the heart of it. But they've got others working for them. Your

roommate, Sid—her Daddy's one of the main suppliers."

"Gosh." I looked over at Sid, who was two girls down from me. "Does she know?"

"No, of course not, she doesn't suspect a thing. So when she's bragging about her family, don't let it get to you. You can actually feel a bit sorry for her."

"What about Amy Glass?"

"Same thing. Her father's in it real big. And she does know. That's why she's not too friendly. She's carrying around a big, dirty secret, and her father says he'll beat her up if she tells." From where I was sitting, I could see Amy's head bent over her homework. She was wearing glasses and looking very studious. I tried to feel sorry for her, having to shoulder such a terrible secret, but it was tough to feel sorry for the Ice Queen.

"The thing is, we need you here, Georgia. You have to keep an eye on things for us."

"For who?"

"The U.S. government. You see, we're close to cracking this particular nut, and we need you to help."

"All right, Jack, I understand, but are you sure you trust me?"

"There's no one I can trust more. You're smart, observant, loyal, and brave."

Right then and there I made a decision. If Beard wasn't really a school, then I didn't have to act as if it were a school. I wouldn't have to speak in any of my classes—except maybe in English—and I wouldn't have to do any of my homework—except maybe for English.

I propped up some books to hide the stamp collection from Tweedy-Bird's beady eyes. I took out a new, unsharpened pencil. If you wanted to sharpen your pencil, the senior girl had told me in the earlier study hall, you raised your hand with the pencil in it and pretended to be sharpening it with the other hand. Whoever was on duty was supposed to acknowledge you and nod his or her head and let you get up.

I raised my hand. Mr. Tweed noticed me right away because his head snapped up, but then his eyes darted back down to his books. I raised my hand up higher, and with my entire arm I began waving the hand that had the pencil in it. Several girls were now staring at me. Mr. Tweed was also staring at me. Feeling my face turn red, I made the ridiculous circular motion with my other hand. Mr. Tweed frowned. He seemed to be debating whether or not he should let me sharpen my pencil. I knew it was difficult to make such an important decision. Finally he nodded. As I got up and walked to the sharpener, I was amazed by the silence in the room. Everyone was working or at least, everyone was being quiet. As I began to sharpen the pencil, a bunch of heads looked up. I guessed watching someone sharpen a pencil must be very fascinating. I could just stand there and grind the pencil all the way to nothing. That would be entertaining. Or, I could stick the eraser end in and grind away, and wouldn't that be fun to watch? Mr. Tweed was glaring at me.

I returned to my desk with a sharp pencil, and at the top of a new page in the People Collection, I wrote "The

Gunrunners' Daughters Series." I had a good view of Sid and Amy. I could do a pretty fair sketch of them.

Ah, now the study hall time flew by.

8:30. Mr. Tweed cleared his throat noisily and dismissed us. The Beard House girls were supposed to walk back to the dorm together. Gabriela had permission to stay on and study more. Abby and Addy, Sid, Amy, Hatty, Lulu, and I left the Dolittle Building together, but as soon as we were outside, Abby and Addy ran on ahead. They seemed to run everywhere they went.

"Call Ross when we get back," Amy said to Sid. (Ross was the adorable brother at St. Andrew's.) "I want to talk to him about Alex." (Alex was the adorable brother's adorable friend.) "Come on, hurry up and get back before Hatty gets the phone." They ran on ahead.

Lulu sang, "I know an old lady who swallowed a fly. I don't know why she swallowed a fly," in a Brooklyn accent at the top of her lungs all the way back to the dorm. Miss Hagman and Mrs. Gross were in the Hag's sitting room just off the front hallway as we trooped in.

The Hag was mending a hem on a uniform skirt, and Grossie was knitting. "Quiet hour is in half an hour and, Lulu, I could hear you a mile away," said the Hag. "Lights out at nine-thirty."

"As if we didn't know," Lulu said out of the side of her mouth.

I hung back in the doorway. I wanted one of the housemothers to say "How was your day, dear?" but they didn't say anything, although Grossie did smile at me over her knitting. And was that a wink? Oh well, a smile and a wink were better than nothing.

"Come on, Gigi," said Lulu. "You can hang out in my room."

Lulu was so nice, and I thought I liked being called Gigi, but I shook my head. I was too tired to hang out with her. Was I going to be this tired at the end of every day at Beard? I went upstairs to my room and put on my pajamas. Amy and Sid were downstairs on the phone, so I didn't have to deal with them.

When I pulled back my bedspread, I found a piece of toffee candy on my pillow. My heart leaped. Gertie! Gertie must have put it there. I held the toffee in my hand. I didn't even want to eat it — I just wanted to hold it.

Then I climbed into bed and played a rousing game of football with Jack, Bobby, and Teddy. I was very agile and clever and fast. The Kennedy brothers were amazed. Then I shut my eyes and drifted into sleep. I didn't even hear Sidney come in.

My first day was over.

I woke up, though, in the middle of the night. I didn't know what woke me up—noises in the old house, creaks and groans? My laundry bag hung like a ghost from my bedpost, and as my eyes grew accustomed to the dark, I saw my school shoes on the floor beside the bed. What had awakened me? Thumps? Above my head? Was there an attic in Beard House? I thought about the old headmistress. Maybe Wilma Beard was wandering around. This had been her house, and she'd be the type who'd want to be a ghost—to keep an eye on her school.

"Everything's okay," said Jack, just as a father ought to when his daughter can't sleep. *"I'm here, watching over you. Go back to sleep."*

"Thanks," I said, and I did go back to sleep.

• • •

Dear Jack,

I have been at Beard for two weeks now. I feel as if I have been here all my life. Mr. Tweed, Miss Payne, Madame Lefèvre, and Miss Pitt have all spoken to me about not doing my homework. I did not say anything while they spoke to me. I just nodded my head.

I was looking at my stamp collection tonight, and Sid and Amy came and hung around. Amy looked at me for a minute and then said, "Don't you ever wish you could grow up?" I ignored her. I have known people like Amy all my life, people who, when they're five, think stuffed animals are babyish, and when they're ten, think you shouldn't pretend anything anymore, and when you're twelve you should start wearing lipstick. And if you scratch your scabs, they are really upset and say don't do that or you'll grow up to have scars. The point is, even when they were five, they could picture themselves as grownups. They could imagine themselves driving cars, getting married, having jobs. What's wrong with me that I can't do that, even now that I'm almost fourteen? The only thing I can imagine about myself when I am grown up is that I will have a refrigerator stuffed with food and there will be no chicken liver pâté in it.

Sid found out my father didn't die. She was really mad at me because I lied about that. She said if I lied about that I could lie about anything.

During the school days things aren't so bad because the day students are nice, although everyone has been at Beard forever and it's hard to break in. I guess I'm not so great at making friends anyway, but having Sid and Amy hate me makes it hard in the dorm. I like Gabriela—at least I don't think she's ever mean, but she seems so grown up and she's always in her room with the door shut and I don't think she wants to be bothered. Addy and Abby are funny and nice, but they seem too young for me. Hatty's whininess and pimpleness get on my nerves. I like Lulu the most. Sid and Amy make fun of me for hanging around with a sixth-grader, but who else am I supposed to hang out with?

From me, agile and clever,
Georgia

7

Every Friday Miss Pearl assigned us a composition for Monday. This Friday she said, Choose a painting and write about it. The walls of her room were covered with prints of paintings. One was called "Christina's World." It was by Andrew Wyeth. On Friday I sat and stared at it for a long, long time, and then I thought that I was the girl lying in the field and that my parents were in the house up on the hill and that I had run away so I didn't have to hear them fighting with each other. The field was quiet, and I could concentrate on each blade of grass and listen to each note of the birds. There were no human voices, only the sky and the grass and the birds and the peace of my own company. So that was what I decided to write about. Only I would not write "I." It would be about Christina, and everything would be "she."

Miss Pearl liked my composition. As she handed it back, she said, "Did you know that Christina can't walk?"

"No," I said. " I hadn't realized that."

"But you realized she was crippled in another way, in her heart."

I felt the inside of my brain click, the way it had when Tim had found just the right word to describe La and Winter. I realized that by writing about Christina, I had learned something about my own feelings. Like how I really felt about my parents' fighting for so many years.

Still holding on to the composition, which had an A at the top, I walked in a daze from English class to recess. An A. I wasn't sure I had ever gotten an A in anything before.

At recess I always went to the mailboxes, although the only letter I had received so far had been from Father Selinsky, welcoming me to the Catholic church.

Why didn't La write to me? Had she dumped me off in

boarding school and then forgotten all about me? I didn't expect Winter to write, but today, what do you know, there was an airmail envelope with a Brazilian stamp on it. The return address was Winter's. I put the Christina composition between my teeth so I could open the letter. Inside the envelope was another airmail envelope, folded so it would fit, and a note in my father's secretary's handwriting. "This was sent here, so I send it on to you. We miss you very much and I hope you are thriving in your new school. Fondly, Alicia Noonan." My eyes filled with tears. How nice of Alicia Noonan to write me a note and to hope I was thriving at my new school. I had always liked Alicia Noonan—a sweet old lady with wrinkles that I had always wanted to touch when I was younger.

Then I looked at the folded envelope. It was addressed to me in a small, neat script, but with no clue as to who had sent it. Well, there was one clue—it had an American stamp. Unfortunately, the postmark was blurry. I took the Christina composition out of my mouth and tucked it into my mailbox and opened the mysterious envelope. There was a single sheet of airmail stationery, what they call onionskin, light and thin. The same small neat handwriting flowed down it in the shape of a poem. My heart began to pound.

"*To Georgia,*" I read.

Girl with wild feet
Leap, fly, jump,
Follow clouds, kiss snakes

Collect stamps, laugh at mirrors
Wish for storms
Hide in always Summer
Because Winter is a grown-up.

Don't forget me,
The Sand Prince

I read the poem ten times. Had Tim written it about me, or for me, or both? Did he mean to make a joke about winter and my father Winter? *Don't forget me,* he had written. When had he written it? Where was he? Why hadn't he put a return address on the envelope?

The bell rang for the end of recess. I folded the Christina composition and the poem and Alicia Noonan's note and put them all into Tim's envelope. I put the envelope into my blazer pocket, where it rested against the moon pebble.

I was so happy for the rest of the day that in science class I even laughed at one of Miss Pitt's jokes. In French class I forgot to be silent and actually answered a question. Everyone stared at me as if they had never seen me before.

• • •

Dear Jack,
It's almost Halloween and Beard House had a pumpkin-carving contest. I carved Grossie's face into my pumpkin and I won. Grossie was one of the judges. She said, "How clever you are, Georgia, that face certainly is ghoulish."

Jack, I know you want me here at Beard to spy on the Bottomley, Tweed, Payne gang, but I haven't seen much activity. I did go down and snoop around the old boathouse yesterday, but I didn't dare go inside and when I looked in the windows, I couldn't see any guns. There's a lot of junk in there and old boats. Maybe the guns are hidden in the boats. Are you sure you really need me to be here?

From the incredible spy,
Georgia M. Hughes

8

Halloween night. Abby and Addy, as the youngest boarders, went over to a day student's house so they could go trick-or-treating. We had to go to study hall. I had been looking forward to going because the last time I got to trick-or-treat, I was eight years old. Lulu was really mad. "They don't let us do anything fun," she said, but I think what she really missed was going out and making a mess of her neighborhood. She told me the stuff she and her friends did every year. I never knew whether or not to believe her stories. She talked like she was a juvenile delinquent, but she was one of the nicest people I had ever known.

At night Superman, a witch, and a clown came to Beard House and stood in the front hallway, and we gave them the candy that Grossie had bought just in case anyone did come. We invited them and their mothers into our living room, and all of us crowded around. I realized it had been a long time since I had seen little kids. Abby and Addy didn't count. I felt as if I had been starved or something—I couldn't stop looking at them.

They liked all the attention we were giving them. Superman began to show off, jumping off chairs, and flying around the room, so his mother said it was time to go. When they left, I wished I had a mother who would hold me by the hand and take me out that door.

Maybe we all felt that way, because the minute they left, we all started jumping off the chairs and flying around the room, everyone except Gabriela. And then Lulu grabbed a mop from the closet and put the stringy part over her head and stuffed a pillow under her shirt and started bossing us around like the Hag.

The next morning I got up early without even waiting for Gertie. I liked seeing her first thing because she always gave me a pep talk. Today I just felt like walking outside. I liked the way the fog rolled up from the river and how the leaves, which were all down now, crunched under my feet, and the air was cold. It was so different from Brazil—the cold, of course, but also how brown and gray and neat everything was. Even the fields and the stone walls seemed neat. Across the way was a pumpkin farm. Through the fog I could see blotches of pinky orange, pumpkins that I figured hadn't been bought for Halloween.

I walked to Dolittle and sat in the hallway, watching the

maids, Mabel and Molly, set the tables for breakfast. I wished I could help them. I liked how they rattled the silverware, crashing down handfuls of forks and knives and spoons on the table, clinking the glasses.

"When I woke up this morning," Mabel was saying to Molly, "I was just laying in bed and I heard this bird outside my window, and I was so surprised. I thought all the birds would be gone by now, but my husband says the phoebes and the chickadees hang around."

"Blue jays, too," Molly said with a laugh. "I have this bird feeder, and you should see the mess the jays make with the bird seed. Bossy birds they are!"

I loved listening to them talk about their lives outside of school. I wished I could see them in their houses, without their maids' uniforms on, and I wondered if people in real life called them Mabel and Molly. They were grownups, weren't they, and didn't they have last names, like Mr. Tweed and Miss Pitt?

And then for the first time ever I had a picture of myself as a grownup. I would live in a yellow house, and in the mornings the sun would stream in the kitchen window and the kitchen would smell like coffee and the refrigerator would be full of food and I wouldn't be attacked by a man with a gun when I opened it.

Now that Halloween was over, kids were talking about Thanksgiving, where they were going to go, what they were going to do. Hatty and Lulu were counting the days. Amy was going to Sid's. Abby and Addy were going back to their small town in New Hampshire. Who knew where Gabriela was going? Back to Spain? And me? No word from La. Well, I would be going to Hyannis, of course, the Kennedy family compound. Everyone would be there. There'd be lots of football on the lawn. John-John and Caroline and all the cousins would be so happy to see me.

9

One Wednesday I found myself staring at Wilma Beard's portrait again on my way to English. What was the school like, I wondered, when Mrs. Beard was running things?

"Why don't you ask her?" A husky voice rang loud and clear in my ears. Yikes.

"Ask who?" I asked

"Miss Pearl, of course," said the voice. *"She was here, she can tell you all about it. She'd be delighted, I can assure you."*

And so, just as the bell for recess rang at the end of the period, instead of going to the mailboxes, I hung back in Miss Pearl's classroom.

"Miss Pearl, I was wondering—"

"Yes?" Miss Pearl cocked her head in that birdlike way she had.

"What was Beard like when Mrs. Beard was the headmistress?"

"Oh, my dear, how delightful that you should ask!" Miss Pearl seemed really pleased. "Wilma was just the most wonderful human being, an inspiration to all who knew her—she took me on as a teacher straight out of college when I still didn't know what I wanted to do. I certainly didn't think I wanted to spend my life with silly schoolgirls—" Miss Pearl laughed her delicate little laugh—"but Wilma showed me that those girls, rather than being silly, were so fresh and interesting and eager to learn. Oh, I was young and rather silly myself in those days." She laughed again. "But she was kind, so kind to me. Oh, my dear, I simply did not know what I was doing."

Miss Pearl was silent for a moment, and I waited. I tried to imagine Miss Pearl as young and just starting out as a teacher, like Miss Fern, perhaps, but it was impossible to think of her as being anything like Miss Fern.

"Were you a housemother?" I asked.

Miss Pearl nodded. "I lived in the loveliest apartment in the attic of Mrs. Beard's home, where you are now. You're not in the attic, of course—I don't believe anyone lives there now. It was before Mr. Beard died—such a nice, gentle, man, so supportive of all of Wilma's ideas, and she did have some extraordinary ideas. I believe Beard was not like other schools," she went on thoughtfully. "Wilma had the most definite ideas about the education of young women. Every Saturday in the fall and the spring, she took the girls up the river in canoes and rowboats, and in the winter we skated."

"Did you go, too?" I asked. I tried to keep the amazement out of my voice.

She laughed. "Oh, yes, indeed. I was quite a strong paddler and a fairly accomplished skater, too."

I smiled. Miss Pearl in a canoe or on skates was as hard to imagine as Miss Pearl on a beach in Rio.

"And Wilma believed young girls should wear comfortable clothing so they could be free to use both their brains and their bodies. They wore blouses and bloomers, most comfortable, I should say. There were two things she could not abide — girls complaining of boredom and girls being mean. The truth was, she kept them so busy working, they really had very little time to be bored or mean. In those days Beard was still a working farm, with cows and vegetables. It's what got us through the war — we were almost completely self-sufficient in those days."

"No maids?" I asked.

Miss Pearl sniffed. "Young women in black dresses and white aprons paid less than minimum wage, waiting hand and foot on healthy girls! No, indeed not! We did have a cook, but everyone had to help in the kitchen — faculty, too. The girls had to make their own beds, clean their rooms, polish their shoes."

"Why isn't Beard like that anymore, Miss Pearl?"

Miss Pearl looked thoughtful again. "Oh, times change, I guess, and Mrs. Beard did become a bit more eccentric as she aged. The school had grown, you understand, during the war years. It was a popular place to educate young women, a place to teach them to be strong and independent, but after the war, I expect girls had to go back to being girls. The school had trustees, and they were beginning to wonder if Mrs. Beard wasn't a bit dotty. They began to think the school should be more like St. Andrew's, that horror of a boys' school across the way. They never fired her, of course. How could they? But they made the last ten years of her life rather unpleasant. I was away doing graduate work myself in those days — Wilma strongly encouraged me — and I have always felt a little selfish that I wasn't here to help her through those days. Then when she died, in 1959, Mr. Bottomley was hired and it was a new era. He has been very kind to me, I should hasten to say, he hired me back here, but —" She seemed to realize suddenly that she was talking to me, a mere student in the school. "Well, the school changed. Proper girls, uniforms, and so on. No more excursions on the river; however, girls are girls whether they are in bloomers or skirts, and as long as there are young, eager, curious minds, and as long as they have good teachers —"

"You," I said.

"Oh, yes, me!" The bell rang then. She began to organize the papers on her desk. "I am simply one of the best teachers on the East Coast." She gave me one of her quick smiles, but I couldn't tell if she was joking or not. "I suppose I have run on," she said. "Thank you for showing an interest, my dear. Not many do, you know."

I went to Miss Pitt's class after that. While she droned on about the different layers of the earth, I thought about girls in bloomers paddling down the Connecticut River.

"Jack, why couldn't I have gone to Beard in the old days?"

"Because we need you here and now. I want you to pay particular attention to Mr. Tweed's tie this week. If he wears the same tie every day, that's a sign that a shipment of guns is coming up the river. It's his way of communicating with Bottomley and Payne."

"Yes, all right, I'll keep a lookout. But I still wish I could have gone to Beard in the old days."

"Ask not what you can do for yourself—"

"I know, I know. I'm with you, Jack, don't worry—I'll be checking out old Tweedy-Bird's tie—"

"Hughes," came a brusque voice. "What causes the blah blah blah?"

I looked at Miss Pitt blankly. "Just as I thought," said Miss Pitt. "Daydreaming as usual. Have you asked yourself what you think you are doing here at Beard? Or are you just another one of those girls Mr. Bottomley has gotten to fill the dormitories?" The girls in the class laughed.

Ha ha, funny, funny, Miss Pitt.

• • •

Dear Jack,

I know exactly what I'm doing here at Beard, and Miss Pitt had better watch out because I'm beginning to wonder about her. Except she's probably too dumb to be part of that conspiracy. It takes some brains to be a good smuggler but no brains to be a bad teacher. That's good, Jack, maybe I should be your speechwriter.

I am beginning to wonder about the Hag, though. She could definitely be part of Things. She's probably the chief torturer. She's hard, with no mercy ever in those steely eyes. If we ever do anything slightly wrong, we have to report to her apartment and sit on her couch, and then she wears us down with the Hag Look.

When Mrs. Gross is on duty (every Tuesday and one weekend a month), we are terrible. We throw food in the TV room and turn the lights back on after lights out and stay up half the night and sneak into the kitchen and steal food.

When we do finally bust the Gun Runners, we should send Mrs. Gross to a nice home where there are no kids, only cats. She is always saying how she would like to have a cat, but Mr. Bottomley won't let her have one.

Sincerely,
Your speechwriter (and daughter),
Georgia M. Hughes

10

One Saturday when Grossie was on duty Amy said, "Let's play Truth or Dare tonight after lights out."

Abby and Addy weren't invited. Too young. Gabriela never did stuff like this. Too smart. Why did I? I knew that anything Amy did, especially something like Truth or Dare, was going to have a nasty side to it. Why did I have to get sucked into Amy's diabolical plans? Because I was weak. Because I thought if I went along with her she might even end up liking me. Why did I want her to like me? I don't know, I don't know, I don't know.

In the dark of night, Sid, Lulu, and I gathered in Hatty and Amy's room. Amy sat in the only chair in the room.

"If you choose Truth, you are asked a question, which you have to answer truthfully," the Queen said. "If you choose Dare, then you have to do a dare. And you have to do it, no matter what. And Hatty," she added in a menacing tone of voice, as Hatty edged toward the door, "anyone who comes in here has to stay in here now. No chickening out."

My heart began to bump in a way that hurt. Amy's tone was not playful. Just like Hatty, I wished I could sneak out. Lulu's dark eyes, on the other hand, were all lit up.

"Start with you, Lu," said Sid, sitting on the arm of Amy's chair. Miss Assistant Queen. "Truth or Dare?"

"I ain't got nothing to hide," Lulu said. "Truth."

Sometimes I thought Lulu said "ain't" on purpose just to shock us.

"Where's your father?" Amy asked. She was in the for the kill, all right. She and Sid exchanged a look. I could see that the two queens had it all planned out—what they were going to ask and what consequences they were going to dish out.

"So," Amy said. "The question has been presented—where's your father, Lu?"

But Lulu was cheerful. "He's in jail," she grinned. "First

for breaking and entering and stuff like that, and then he hit a cop. Almost killed him. I ain't never seen him." She shrugged her shoulders. "I don't care. I ain't ashamed, if that's what you guys want me to be. I wouldn't even be at this lah-di-dah school if it wasn't for some do-gooder lady who's payin' to send me here. Anything else you'd like to know?"

Everyone just sat and stared at Lulu. Even Amy didn't seem to know what to say for a moment. Lulu smiled and inspected her nails. (The ones on her left hand were pink and the ones on her right hand were red.)

Then Amy looked at me and my heart started bumping again. "Well, Miss Hughes, Truth — or Dare?"

The Truth was, I didn't want any of them to know the smallest thing about me. No, I wouldn't talk. Go ahead — chop off my legs, push splinters under my fingernails. (Mine weren't any color, just a little bit chewed.)

"Truth," I heard myself saying.

"Have you ever been kissed by a boy, and by who and when?" Amy asked with a smirk.

"That's more than one question," Hatty said.

Everyone in the room stared at Hatty. Fancy meek and mild Hatty speaking up like that! Amy looked surprised, but then she shrugged. Hatty was like a fly to her — annoying but harmless.

I looked around. They were all staring at me — they all wanted to know, except Hatty, maybe, who couldn't care less about boys. Too bad for them they had hit upon the one thing I would never tell them, not in a million years.

Amy squinted at me. Such terrible eyes for one so young. She looked like she was forty, squinting like that. Then I knew what Amy's problem was—she had never been a kid. She had been born forty years old and had to walk around pretending she was younger. "Come on, out with it," she said.

I thought of Tim and New Year's Eve. I thought of the pebble. I wished I had it in my pocket right now. I remembered how new Tim's shirt smelled when he leaned toward me and how surprised I was when he kissed me.

No, I was not going to tell about that time. They would never know about Tim.

"I'll take a dare," I said.

Amy laughed.

"Don't," said Hatty. "You don't have to do any of this, Georgia." She was standing against the wall near the door. Was this really whiny, sniffly Hatty?

"Here's the dare," Amy said, ignoring her. "Tomorrow night when Tweedy-Bird is on duty, you have to run through evening study hall naked." Sid laughed a wild laugh and Lulu giggled. I even smiled, because I couldn't believe Amy was serious. "I'm not kidding," she said. "You have to, because that's the game, and if you don't, you're going to be sorry."

"You're not going to make her do that," Hatty said.

"Hey, that's way too embarrassing," Lulu said. "I mean, with Tweedy-Bird there? That's not even funny—I mean, some dares are funny, but—"

"A dare's a dare," said Amy.

"And you're a jerk," I said. I got up and walked out of the room and slammed the door behind me. I hoped Grossie would hear it and come running. My face was burning and my chest hurt. I ran down the hall to the River Room and, without undressing, crawled into bed and pulled the covers over my head. If I closed my eyes very tight I could be at the cottage in Búzios but oh, no, someone was creeping into the room.

"Georgia?"

It was Hatty. I recognized her feeble voice. Or was it so feeble? She had been brave in the glare of Amy's squinty eyes. But I didn't want her pimply sympathy right now. I kept my eyes squeezed shut and pretended to be asleep. "Don't let her get to you, okay?" she said, and then she was gone.

I imagined I was floating in the warm sea, floating, floating, without a worry in the world. I fell into a deep sleep and never even heard Sid come in.

"Georgia. Georgia Hughes," a voice was saying. *"Wake up, I want to talk to you."* My eyes flew open. Where was I? Not in Búzios. It was too cold. The radiator was making weird ticking noises. *"Georgia Hughes, I want to tell you that Amy Glass is just full of hot air, you know. You must ignore her."*

Who was speaking to me? A shiver ran up my back. It was Mrs. Beard, it had to be—no one was around, and anyway, I recognized her voice.

"She's trying to get your goat because you have something she doesn't have."

"What do I have that she doesn't have?" Here it was, the middle of the night, and I was talking to Mrs. Beard.

"Think," said Mrs. Beard.

I sat up in bed and in the middle of the night tried to think. What did I have that Amy didn't have? Amy had a ton of friends—she got invited to day students' houses, she had friends who were juniors and seniors, and besides that, boys from St. Andrew's were always calling her up. She was in all the top classes, which meant she was smart. She was really good at field hockey, and she was one of Miss Pitt's pets. Miss Pitt even invited her over to her apartment. Sometimes both Amy and Sid would have dinner with her, and then come back bragging about all the good food they'd had.

What did I have that Amy didn't have?

Boobs. Amy was flat-chested.

Also a photograph of John F. Kennedy.

A stamp collection.

"Yes," said Mrs. Beard.

"Yes, what?"

"Your stamp collection."

"My stamp collection?" I started to laugh.

"What I mean is," said Mrs. Beard. *"Well, never mind what I mean. Now, about running through that study hall—"*

"I'm not going to do it, Mrs. Beard, don't worry."

"Splendid," she said. I fell back to sleep.

In the morning I thought about what Mrs. Beard had said, or what I thought she had said. My stamp collection?

I looked at Jack. "How come you're not giving me advice?" I asked.

"Because Mrs. Beard has a good head on her shoulders."

"Yeah, I guess," I said.

• • •

Dear Jack,

This has been the worst week of my life. I got sent to Mr. Tweed's office by Miss Payne because I have not been doing my work. He said, "Now, Miss Hughes, if you keep this up we are going to have to take Steps." I just sat there and nodded and looked at his tie. Tweedy-Bird has worn the same tie four days in a row. It is red with squiggles on it that are shaped like a C. Red for communism. C for Cuba. It must be the signal.

Amy and Sid aren't speaking to me. They come into the room and pretend I'm not there. Amy says things like, "I hate kids who lie," and Sid says, "Yeah." Then Amy says, "I hate rich kids who are stuck up and think they're better than anyone else," and Sid says, "Yeah." I know they are talking about me. I pretend I don't care, but I do. I mean, I don't think I want to be friends with them, but I've never been hated before—at least I don't think I have. I don't see what I did that was so bad. I don't see why I should tell them about Tim, and I don't see why I have to feel bad about refusing to run naked through study hall—I mean, would Sid or Amy ever do that? I try to remember what you said about their fathers—Sid's and Amy's—

how they are in the gunrunning operation. When I remember that, I don't feel so bad about them. Sid and Amy are over at Miss Pitt's apartment right now and I am so glad. They won't be back until after supper. Well, I have to go now. Lulu wants me to help her bleach her hair.

Sincerely yours,
Your lying daughter,
Georgia

11

A rainy Saturday in November. I looked out the window and what I saw was so different from anything I ever saw from my window in Rio. Where were the palm trees? All I could see here were trees with these bare bony finger kind of branches scraping away at the gray sky. Why was the sky always gray in November?

After Saturday study hall, we went on an X. That is Beard lingo for EXpedition. They tried to broaden our education by taking us on these enrichening experiences. This time they put us all on a bus and took us to Gillette Castle. It actually was a neat place, built by an actor named William Gillette, who became famous for playing Sherlock Holmes.

The best thing was it looked like one of those drippy castles you make out of wet sand, and I suddenly remembered how Tim said the Sand Prince's castle was made of sand. I walked around being the Sand Princess and pretended I was playing Stalk the Enemy with the Sand Prince. I really felt as if he were in the castle somewhere. I didn't want to leave—it made me feel less bad about Sid and Amy, somehow, as if they didn't matter.

On the way back to school, I sat with Lulu and Hatty in the front of the bus. Lulu tried to teach us how to talk with a Brooklyn accent, and we laughed like maniacs. There were older girls sitting all around us, laughing at us laughing, and they teased Lulu about her hair. The bleaching had made it come out in stripes, and she looked like a skunk. Hatty was actually fun on this trip, maybe because no one could be draggy when Lulu was around and maybe because Sid and Amy were at the back of the bus and we forgot about them and didn't care how we acted.

On Sunday it was still raining. I went to church and stared at the hat of a woman who was sitting in front of me and tried to think about what I would write for Miss Pearl's Monday composition. It was supposed to be about something that had happened to me. Well, nothing had ever happened to me. I couldn't think of a single thing to write about. I was a very boring person.

After Sunday dinner, I went up to my room to try to think about the composition again when Sid and Amy rushed in.

"Come on, Georgia, we want to show you something," said Amy.

"Up in the attic, it's really neat," said Sid.

I remembered that Miss Pearl had lived in the attic of Beard House, and I thought that was what Sid and Amy wanted to show me. Silly me. I didn't stop to wonder why they were suddenly being so friendly. It did flit across my mind that maybe they were sorry for the way they had been treating me and had decided they were going to be friends with me now.

Just across the hall from the River Room was a door I had always assumed led to a closet. Sid opened it and switched on a light and to my surprise I was facing a flight of stairs.

"Come on," she said, and she and Amy started up the stairs.

I followed after them. At the top was an actual room, low-ceilinged but cozy, with an old desk, an armchair, and two beds.

"It even has a sink and a potty," said Amy, pulling back a curtain to show a tiny bathroom. "I wouldn't mind living up here."

"I would," said Sid with a shiver. "It gives me the creeps. I think Mrs. Beard's ghost lives up here."

"Whooooo, whoooo, I am the ghost of Wilma Beard!" Amy flapped around the room acting demented, and the next thing I knew, both Sid and Amy were running down the stairs screaming with laughter. The attic light went off and the door slammed, and then there was silence.

So they had played a trick on me. Just when I thought they had started to like me. I should have known. How could I have ever believed for a moment that Amy wanted to be friends with me? My face felt all hot with stupidity, and my insides were icy with anger. I hated those girls, I really did.

There were windows in the attic, and a kind of sad rainy afternoon light came through them. I could see enough to make my way down the stairs. I tried the door, but it wouldn't open. I pushed against it, my throat tight, my heart hammering, but the door wouldn't budge. They had locked it from the outside. Leaning against the door, I tried to think. Well, I wasn't going to give them the satisfaction of screaming or banging on the door. I could practically hear them breathing on the other side, just waiting, covering up their giggles. They reminded me of Ruthie and Elizabeth. Stupid girls, Tim would have said.

I tiptoed back upstairs. Something brushed against my hair and I wanted to scream. Looking up, I saw a string hanging from a light bulb. With a yank, the light came on. Stumbling onto one of the beds, I looked around, trying to think.

Sid and Amy had brought me up here to lock me in a place they thought was creepy, but they were wrong—it was nice in the attic. It had some junk in it, suitcases and trunks, somebody's violin case, a bunch of moldy stuffed animals, skis and ski boots, but I saw that it could be a great place to live. The beds were made up and had blankets folded at the ends of them. Maybe after Miss Pearl no longer lived there, the room had been used when there were more boarders at Beard House.

No, the attic wasn't bad, and I wasn't afraid of Mrs. Beard. After all, Mrs. Beard talked to me and looked out for me. It was Sid and Amy who were the problem. Amy, really. Sid on her own wasn't so bad, but she was a different person when she was with Amy.

Why did Amy hate me so much? I hadn't done anything to her except be Sid's roommate and that wasn't my fault.

"Stamp collection," said a voice.

I looked around, hoping that this time I might actually see Mrs. Beard, but the voice was inside my head, as clear as anything.

"She wants your stamp collection," she said.

"Why? Why would she want my stamp collection?"

"That is for you to find out," said Mrs. Beard. *"But meanwhile, someone ought to be making those girls rake leaves so they'll stop being so tiresome. I really should speak to Miss Pearl."*

"Do you?" I asked. "Speak to Miss Pearl?"

"Often," she said. *"Now, my dear, if you want to play a good trick back on those two girls, this is what you must do. There is a maple tree growing right outside of the house. You just have to open the window, climb out, shut the window again, scurry down the tree, and go right back into the dormitory. They'll never know how you got out."*

I grinned and jumped up from the armchair and nearly knocked myself out on one of the beams that sloped overhead.

"Sorry about that," said Mrs. Beard. *"Old houses are like that, you know. Turn the light out before you go. No sense in running up the electricity bill."*

I turned off the light and made my way over to the window. At first I couldn't get it open, but with some banging I got it to move. Outside, just within reach, was a branch of the maple tree. It was still raining, which was good, because it meant it wasn't likely that anyone would be outside or would look out a window and see me in the tree.

I leaned out and grabbed the branch and swung my body out. I had had plenty of practice at things like that, traveling along the outside of the balcony in Rio, millions of meters up. My bare feet would tingle with the thrill of it. I felt that same thrill up the back of my neck now, and besides that, I felt laughter bubbling up inside at the thought of Sid and Amy.

I reached back and shut the window. Then I hugged the tree in a rush of sheer happiness. The air was fresh with rain and the sharp smell of rotting leaves. I felt wild and free, the way I used to feel at night on the balcony. Then I began to climb down.

I climbed right past Mrs. Gross's bedroom. Her light was on, and I could see clearly into the room. There was a bed, a painting of a vase of flowers over the bed, a desk with a cup and saucer on it, an electric teapot on a bookshelf. Grossie was in an armchair, reading, in her bathrobe and slippers. She was wearing a red turban on her head, but her hair was down, her long, scraggly, black-and-white-striped hair. She was pretty hideous.

I thought with a pang that her room wasn't any better than mine in the Tower—perhaps it was even a bit smaller.

The terrible thing was, Grossie was old, and this was all she had. And then laughter threatened to spill out of me again. I could scare the living daylights out of old Grossie by tapping on the window—scare the teeth right out of her head. I pictured her teeth chattering away by themselves in midair.

Grossie, I will spare you this time, but if you ever give me a hard time, I know exactly what I'll do.

On Sunday nights we stayed in our dorms for supper. As I neared the bottom of the tree, I looked through the kitchen window and could see the Hag standing at the counter stirring something in a bowl. Probably chocolate pudding. On Sunday nights, dessert was always chocolate pudding. Lulu was twirling around the kitchen with a wooden spoon in her hand. Lulu never was good at helping. The Hag was always saying to her, "Lulu you're going to have to be rich when you grow up and have lots of servants to wait on you," and Lulu always said, "You betcha I'm gonna be rich." Abby and Addy were putting dishes and silverware on trays. Gabriela was sitting at the table, reading—didn't that girl ever stop? And where was Hatty? On the phone, probably—she was always homesick on Sunday nights.

Most importantly, Sid and Amy weren't there. I bet they were up in the attic looking for me. Ha! I bet they were panicked! What if I never showed up and they had to admit what they'd done—then they'd get into wicked trouble. It was almost worth not going in, letting them sweat a bit, but I was hungry, and besides, I couldn't wait to see the expressions on their faces.

I swung down from the last branch and ran for the door. I hoped no one would notice that my clothes were splotchy from the rain. I raced into the house, took a deep breath, and made the plunge. I walked into the kitchen.

12

"Oh, there you are, Gigi," said Lulu. "I've been looking everywhere for you."

"You will do all the dishes tonight," the Hag said coldly. "Including the pots and pans. The idea of coming down so late!"

The Hag could tell me to scrub the whole kitchen floor for all I cared because at that moment Sid and Amy came into the kitchen and stared at me as if I were a ghost. Ha! I loaded up my plate with the every-Sunday-night corn fritters, still hot from the oven, and doused them with a ton of maple syrup, making up for all the years I didn't have maple syrup in Brazil.

On Sunday nights we could eat anywhere downstairs in the house. Usually I followed Lulu to wherever she wanted to eat, but tonight I struck out on my own. I was the leader now. I went to one of the sitting rooms, and Lulu followed me. Hatty, red-eyed and weepy, found us. Not far behind were Sid and Amy. Lulu raised her eyebrows at them. "How come they're eating with us?" she muttered.

"They think we're great," I said.

"Since when?" Lulu asked. Her plate of food tipped dangerously.

"Watch out," I said. "You're dripping maple syrup on me." For the first time I felt older than Lulu. Hatty and Lulu and I sat on the floor, and Sid and Amy sat down in the room's two biggest chairs. Still playing at being Queens, but I knew I wasn't afraid of them anymore.

"Where've you been, Gigi?" Lulu asked. "I've been looking everywhere for you."

"In the attic," I said, looking directly at Sid and Amy.

"In the attic? What were you doing up there?"

"Checking out a ghost."

"Yeah, right, Gigi." Lulu was a kid who went in for gangs, not for ghosts.

"What happened?" Amy asked.

"What do you mean?" I asked, all sweet and innocent.

"I mean—how'd you—"

"How'd I what?"

"First you were behind us and then you weren't." Amy was smooth, all right. "Why'd you stay up there?"

"Stay up where?"

"In the attic." No doubt about it, Amy was getting mad.

"I didn't stay," I said.

"But how?"

"How what?" I thought Amy might slide off her chair and come over and crack me on the head with her plate of corn fritters. Sid sat, plate on her lap, but she wasn't eating. She kept tugging on her ponytail and then pulling off the elastic, twisting her hair, and putting the hair back into the ponytail. I figured she was worried she was going to get into wicked trouble. Maybe Daddy the Trustee would find out about this—maybe locking her roommate in the attic hadn't been such a great thing to do.

"Gigi was checking out the ghost," Lulu said.

"Is there really a ghost?" Hatty asked, sniffing. She always sniffed a lot on Sunday nights. "Whose ghost?"

"Mrs. Beard," I said. "You know, Wilma Beard, who started this school. This used to be her house. She lives in the attic."

"Really?" Hatty's red eyes were wide. She had a mouthful of fritters, which in her amazement she stopped chewing.

I, meanwhile, chewed happily. The fritters were soggily perfect from the syrup. "I actually saw her up in the attic this afternoon, after you guys left," I said, nodding at Sid and Amy. "That's why I didn't come down right away."

"You're cuckoo, nutso," said Lulu, crossing her eyes at me.

"What did she look like?" Hatty asked.

"I didn't get a good look at her—you know, ghosts aren't that easy to see, but I expect she has white hair and all that. Like her picture, you know, the one in Dolittle."

"What did she do?" Hatty asked. "Did she spook you or anything?"

"Of course not, she's a really nice ghost. She likes kids."

"You're talking like this really happened," Amy said.

"How do you know it didn't?" I asked. "You weren't there."

Amy looked away. Ha.

"So did you talk to her?" Amy asked, a cool edge to her voice.

"Well, we did talk for a while. She talked about how when girls were mean she used to make them rake leaves."

Amy, Sid, Hatty, and Lulu sat and stared at me. Hatty really believed me. Lulu thought I was cuckoo, nutso. Amy and Sid, I was pretty sure, thought I was making it all up—lying, as usual—and they didn't like it.

"Did you know the girls here used to go canoeing on the river?" I asked. "Miss Pearl used to go with them."

"Neat," said Lulu, really impressed.

"I knew that," said Hatty. "My mother loved canoeing on the river. It was one of her favorite memories of Beard."

"But how—when—did you leave?" Sid asked. It was costing her, having to ask. She hadn't touched her food at all.

"Well, after a while I went down the stairs, but I couldn't open the door. It was stuck for some reason."

"That's terrible," Hatty said. "I would have died being stuck up in that attic by myself."

"How come you didn't call out for help?" Amy asked. "I mean, Sid and I were right there in the River Room, and we didn't hear you."

I scraped my fork back and forth across my plate, trying

to get the last bits of syrup. Everyone cringed at the sound. "Well, Mrs. Beard came back, and she went through the door and let me out."

"She went through the *door*?" Sid looked shaken.

"Of course," I said. "She's a ghost."

"Are you crazy or are you a really good liar?" Amy blurted out.

"She's nutso," Lulu said cheerfully.

"Liar," Amy said, but not loudly.

"Let's get some chocolate pudding." I said "chocolate" in my best Brooklyn accent and danced out of the room. I helped myself to a huge helping of pudding under the evil eye of the Hag, who was still annoyed at me for not helping to prepare the meal.

• • •

Dear Jack,

I just finished writing the best composition of my life. I'm calling it "Locked in the Attic." I disguised the names of the not-so-innocent. Amy is Buffy, Sid is Muffy. And it is the first time since I have been at Beard that I feel really happy.

From your incredible daughter,
Georgia

13

Miss Pearl gave back my "Locked in the Attic" comp. There was no grade on it. She said, "You were supposed to write about something that really happened to you."

"It really did happen to me," I said.

"You were locked in an attic and Mrs. Beard talked to you?"

"Yes," I said. "And actually she told me she talks to you. Does she?"

Miss Pearl turned away slightly, and I couldn't see her face. When she turned back, she said, "Georgia Hughes, you are brave and resourceful and a good writer to boot."

She wrote A at the top of the composition.

Miss Pearl thought I was a good writer. And she thought I was brave and resourceful. No one had ever told me that before. No one had ever told me anything before about what I was like. I had just sort of floated through my life not knowing anything about myself. I wondered if there was a me to discover, or if I could actually choose how I wanted to be?

The best things about the Beard School were Mrs. Beard and Miss Pearl. And Gertie.

One morning Gertie wanted to know why I had a picture of JFK. I said it was because I really liked him, and she said she did, too. She called him the handsome young Irish president (she was Irish too), and she said he helped people, like trying to integrate the schools. It was funny that Gertie was the only person in the whole school who ever talked about what was happening in the world. I mean, World War Three could have been going on and we wouldn't have known it. Every morning she told me the news, and every night she left a piece of candy for me under my pillow.

"How long have you worked here?" I asked her one time.

"Three years," she said.

"Is it hard?"

I don't think anyone had ever asked her that before. She looked kind of puzzled, and then she said, "It's hard seeing young girls like you so far away from their families. Doesn't seem right. When the girls are rude, and they are sometimes, I know it's only because they don't know any better. It's not their fault—they just haven't been raised right. Now you, you've been taught some manners, I can see that. What a nice family you must come from." She stood there shaking her head. "All the way from Brazil! Imagine that! Now what's a nice girl like you doing so far from home?"

I swallowed hard. I didn't want Gertie to know I didn't come from the greatest family. I tried to think of what to say.

"It was the school in Brazil" is what I finally said. "It wasn't so great, and my parents wanted me to get a good education, so they had to send me away." Well, it sort of was like that, but maybe Amy was right. Maybe I was just a liar, through and through. Gertie pressed my arm and smiled and said, "There, you see, I knew there must be a good reason. My, they surely must miss you."

When Sid found out that Gertie gave me candy, she started being chatty to her—phony nice. Sid could really turn on the charm, and some of the teachers, Miss Pitt, especially, were fooled by her, but Gertie didn't seem to be falling for it. So far, anyway, no candy was turning up under Sid's pillow.

Sid, in general, seemed to be having a hard time. She and Amy were having these little spats—something to do with the adorable brother, Ross, and his adorable friend, Alex. I knew that much because I had overheard Sid wailing away to Ross on the phone one night after Amy had stormed out of our room and yelled something about how she didn't like Ross anyway because he was stuck up like all the Callahans.

One night after study hall, Lulu and I were hacking around for awhile in her room, listening to Peter, Paul, & Mary, pretending our hockey sticks were guitars, and flipping our hair around like folk singers, when all of a sudden we heard Amy and Sid screaming at each other. Then there was this huge slamming of a door. We went out in the hallway and found everyone but Sid and Amy out there, too, even Gabriela.

"They had a big fight," said Hatty, looking scared.

Then it was nine o'clock, quiet hour, and we all had to go to our rooms. When I walked into the River Room, Sid was on her bed. Her face was red and blotchy.

"Is something wrong, Sid?" I asked, sitting on my bed.

"No," she said. (Loud sniff.)

"Did you and Amy have a fight?"

"Sort of," she said. (Loud sniff.) "I mean, yes, we did. It started over something stupid. I borrowed her hockey kilt and then I couldn't find it and she got really mad and said I always borrow her things but never return them. Then she said it wasn't just the clothes, but that I was self-centered and I was always bragging about my brother and my family." (Loud sniff.) "And then, well, Ross has this friend, Alex, and they've been coming over in a canoe to meet us. We meet them down on the dock, you know, and you'd better not tell anyone, Georgia, not Lulu, or anyone. I mean, this place is so small and everyone talks, and if we get found out I'll get into trouble and Daddy will be furious. Well, anyway, about Amy—I said, 'If you think I'm self-centered, well, I think you're a wicked flirt,' and I told her how she flirts all over the place with Alex even though she knows I like him, even when she knows my brother Ross likes *her,* but she still flirts with Alex right under Ross's nose, right under my nose—she isn't happy unless she has all the guys liking her—well, so then she called me a bitch and slapped me across the face."

There was a red mark on Sid's face and it made me feel sick.

"I want to go and live in Grady," she said, starting to cry. "I hate this stinking dorm, I really do."

"I'd miss you, Sid," I said, and at that moment I really did feel that way. I mean, I sure didn't want Sid to leave, because then I'd probably end up with Amy as my roommate.

Sid looked surprised. "Geez," she said, "I didn't even think you liked me. I mean, you never talk to me or tell me anything."

"You mean I wouldn't tell you who I kissed and all that stuff?" I said, beginning to get mad.

Sid laughed. "Look, I'm not trying to pick a fight with you, Georgia. One fight a night is enough. I just think it would be nice if you talked more. You keep everything to yourself."

"Oh," I said, which wasn't a helpful thing to say, but I couldn't think of anything else right at that moment. Then I said, "Are you going to tell Miss Hagman that Amy slapped you?"

"Are you kidding? You know how much trouble she'd get into?"

"Don't you want her to?"

"You can't rat on your friends."

"Oh, she's your friend," I said, sarcastically. "I didn't know friends slapped each other."

"Oh, sure they do, sometimes. At least, they fight sometimes. Like Ross and I do—the brother-sister thing, you know."

"I guess I don't know. I don't have brothers and sisters," I said. I couldn't tell her about Caroline and John-John, and besides, I didn't fight with them. And I didn't want to tell her I hated fighting and raised voices and screaming and yelling because of Winter and La.

But now Sid's eyes were all lit up. "Once Ross and I had

this really bad fight. He went to slug me and I ducked and his fist smashed into the door and he broke his wrist." She laughed her wacko laugh. "Can you imagine what would have happened if I hadn't ducked? He would've smashed my face."

She laughed again, and I said, "We'll get the Hag in here for sure if you keep laughing like that."

"Naw, she can't hear us, she's too old." Then she said, "I wonder if she and Grossie ever fight. Just scream and whale into each other. What do you think?"

"Grossie's teeth would fall out," I said.

"Her wig would fall off."

"Her eyelashes would fall out."

"Her head would fall off."

We both started to laugh so hard I thought for sure both Grossie and the Hag would come running. I wished Sid and Amy would fight more often. It was fun being friends with Sid.

"Georgia," she said suddenly. "How did you get out of the attic?"

I looked at her a minute. I wanted to tell her, I really did. I wanted to be friends with her and tell her things. "I don't think you'll believe me," I said.

"I will, I promise, " she said. "And I won't tell Amy, either. And I'm real sorry we did what we did."

"Well, Mrs. Beard did help me."

Sure enough, Sid got mad. She huffed at me and said, "Come on, Georgia, don't start that again."

"But she did," I said.

"I'm going to bed," she said. "I don't know why I have a roommate who always lies." She huffed around some more and put on her pajamas and spat a lot into the sink while she was brushing her teeth. Then she turned the light off on her side and got into bed and pulled the covers over her head.

• • •

Dear Jack,
Here I am sitting and writing to you because you're the only one I can tell things to. I wonder what it would be like to have a mother I could tell things to. I wonder what would happen if I wrote letters to La instead of to you.

Your loving daughter,
Georgia

14

That night I dreamed I was in a boat and my mother was standing on the shore yelling something to me about the hat I was wearing. The wind was coming up and La was yelling louder and louder.

I woke up with a start. My mother's voice had sounded so clearly in my ears, as if she were standing next to me. And in the middle of the night I began to think about La, and how it must have been for her to come home and find out that Winter had taken up with Lucinda.

Had her heart frozen the way mine had when I realized Amy and Sid had played a trick on me? Had her insides turned to ice?

I thought again of how the entire time we were in Washington, La had been on the phone with her lawyer, smoking cigarette after cigarette. She had forgotten to buy clothes for me. All that was a sign, wasn't it, that La was having a hard time? And she hadn't written, not one single letter. Maybe she was ill. It was that cough. La always said it was asthma, but maybe it was lung cancer. And except for Dorothy, my mother was alone now, all alone.

I sat up in bed and turned on my flashlight. I reached out and rummaged around on my desk until I found pen and paper. My mother needed me. I would be a comfort to her. I would write and let her know that all was well at boarding school. I would not give her one moment of worry. La didn't need to know I was having a hard time with Amy Glass. And La didn't need to know that I wasn't working (except in English), because Beard wasn't really a school.

Dear La,

You are probably wondering how things are going. Well, pretty good. Sidney, my roommate, the girl you thought was so attractive is [Here I had to think for a moment] *still attractive. The food is pretty good here, wholesome and nourishing. We went to a neat castle,*

Gillette Castle. It was built by a famous actor who played Sherlock Holmes. So we do educational stuff on the weekends. English is the best. Miss Pearl, the English teacher, throws our comps up in the air and says, "These papers are the worst I have ever read. They are a cocktail of nothing. Except for this one written by Miss Hughes that is strong drink indeed and restores one's faith in humanity." La, I hope you are good and that you aren't smoking so much.

Your loving daughter,
Georgia

I put the letter into an envelope, addressed it, sealed it, turned off the flashlight, and lay back in bed. Another idea was stealing across my brain. It was time to turn over a new leaf. I needed to start doing well in school for my poor mother's sake. La probably hadn't really wanted to send me away to boarding school—she just knew she had to. From now on I would raise my hand in all my classes, except for math, which really was a muddle, but maybe I could go to Miss Payne and ask for help. And I would do all my homework.

I looked up at Jack. I couldn't make out his face too well in the dark room, but I whispered to him, "I have to start doing my homework because even if Beard is just pretending to be a school, I'll blow my cover if I don't start acting like I think it's a school, too."

Jack didn't answer.

"Jack?"

The radiator ticked away, and somewhere above me the house creaked. *"For heaven's sakes, stop talking and go to sleep,"* said Mrs. Beard, *"or you'll be no use to anyone."*

I closed my eyes and fell back to sleep.

15

Tweedy-Bird and Miss Pitt and Madame were astonished by my great curiosity and new eagerness for learning. At least they certainly acted surprised. And I did my homework all week. Except for math, but that's another story. As it turned out, the work, except for math, wasn't so hard, just soooooo, soooooo boring. I even made an effort in field hockey. Instead of drifting to the back the way I usually did, I stuck by Miss Fern's side as she tried to organize us, and I helped her pass out pinnies.

At the breakfast and supper table, I decided to sit next to Mrs. Tweed. She was this limp, straggly person with limp, straggly hair who taught sewing to the sophomores, and from what I heard they tortured her. Usually everyone avoided sitting next to her because she was always so glum and talked only if she wanted you to pass the salt or the gravy. But I was going to turn over a new leaf. Not only was I going to work hard, I was going to stand up for the weak and downtrodden, like Miss Fern and Hatty and Mrs. Tweed. When La sat next to a quiet person at a dinner party, she hammered them with questions and got them talking, so I figured I could do the same thing with Mrs. Tweed.

I started by asking her how long she and Mr. Tweed had been at Beard. She sighed and said four years. Then I asked her how come they were here, and she sighed and said it was because Mr. Tweed got tired of mowing the lawn and painting the house and he didn't have to do any of those things here. Then I asked her where she had lived before, and she sighed and said some place not far from Beard where she had raised cocker spaniels, and I asked her if she still raised cocker spaniels, because I couldn't remember having seen any at the school, and she said, "No, because Mr. Bottomley would never permit dogs in the dormitories."

Then I thought about the gunrunning to Cuba. Poor Mrs. Tweed probably didn't know anything about that, and I felt so sorry for her. Mr. Tweed's mustache was probably some sort of stupid disguise. I felt like pulling it off.

Now about math and Miss Payne. The Payne. She was the biggest Pain I ever met. She was also the squarest-shaped woman I had ever seen—the Hag was pretty bad, but the Payne was worse. She always wore gray suits, and she was large and square on top with toothpick legs. I always wondered how those little toothpicks supported her. She had steel gray hair just like the Hag—they must have gone to the same hairdresser. Maybe they were sisters. But the Payne was balding. I could see her pink scalp—it reminded me of baby mice.

She was the most boring boring boring boring woman alive. Imagine leeches all over your body, slimy and rubbery, impossible to scrape off. That was how my skin felt the entire time I was in her class. By the end I was sucked dry—there was no blood in me at all and I could barely stand up. I didn't see how she could be in this gunrunning conspiracy, because she was so boring the Cubans wouldn't even want to deal with her, unless she just sat in the back of the room polishing the guns or something.

And what's more, I had come to hate *x*, the stupid unknown quantity. If you want to know, *x* really is *known*—*x* really does have a name. Why should it go around calling itself *x*?

What if I went around calling myself *x*? What if I said, my father's name is Winter and my mother's name is La, so Winter plus La = *x*. Now figure out my real name. How would anyone ever be able to do that?

Or what if I said *x* minus Winter = La?

Or would it be *x* divided by Winter = La?

Or what happened if you added a beautiful Brazilian woman to the equation and subtracted La? What did that do to *x*, to me, Georgia Hughes?

Well, the Payne didn't know. She just stood there and droned on and on about *x*.

When I went to her and asked for help, she said, "If you

paid more attention in class I would be happy to help you. But until you do, I am afraid you will have to swim against the current by yourself."

• • •

Dear Jack,
The best thing right now is that every night after lights out, Sid and I have this whole thing where she pretends to be the Hag and I pretend to be Grossie and we laugh so hard. The worst thing is that during the day, if Sid is with Amy, she totally ignores me. Is she a friend or not?

Is Tim a friend? And where is he?

Are you a friend?

Your friend and daughter,
Georgia

16

For a solid week there was a flurry of testing. It gradually dawned on me that the tests were related to midterm grades. Then Mr. Tweed had all the boarders come into his classroom during a recess, and one by one he handed each girl a report card. I was shocked. The school that wasn't a school was turning out to be a school. I went out into the hallway and forced myself to look at my report card.

Georgia Hughes Grade 8 Fall Term 1963

History: F. If Miss Hughes thinks she can disguise her slovenly performance by several days of grade grubbing, she is sadly mistaken — H. Tweed

Pre-Algebra: F. I must ask what this student thinks she is doing at this school. At this time she is merely occupying a desk — M. Payne

Science: F. Poor to little understanding of tectonic plates, although has begun to show some potential — P. Pitt

English: A. Splendid! — I. Pearl.

French: D. Oh la la! Mlle is not completely with us — Y. Lefevre

Physical Education: C. Georgia needs to work on her attitude in field hockey — S. Fern

Art: B. Georgia needs to work on her attitude in art — S. Fern

Housekeeping: Satisfactory. Georgia takes good care of her belongings — B. Hagman

Dormitory: Georgia needs to spend more time with girls her own age. She needs to spend less time with younger girls — B. Hagman

Girls clustered in the hallway, holding on to their cards. All around me they were saying, "What'd you get? What'd you get?"

I felt as if I were burning up. My hands were sweaty. What a place. You couldn't keep anything to yourself in this school.

I staggered to the mailbox. Maybe Tim had sent me another poem. I needed a poem from him. But oh, what a surprise — there was a letter from my mother. I recognized her heavy, square handwriting that sloped to the left, as if the words didn't really want to go across the page. And La's trademark, her turquoise blue fountain pen ink. It stood out on her nice new light blue stationery — very elegant. I tore open the envelope.

Georgia,

I am sorry to say I am appalled on several counts. I have received your shocking report card. Honestly, Georgia, pull yourself together and for heaven's sakes, act your age. You don't need to associate so much with the younger girls. And if you cannot pull your grades up by the end of term, we shall have to think of what to do. It is not inexpensive for your father to send you to Beard.

While I am glad the school food is good, I hope you are not eating too much of it. We shall need to do some shopping together when you come home for Thanksgiving. I am afraid I sent you off with rather a sparse wardrobe.

Please do get on with it, Georgia. Weather is damp here and Dorothy lately has been impossible. I'm afraid I might have to replace her.

Yours, La (Mother)

P. S. I am sending back your letter with the slang circled. "Pretty good," "neat," "stuff." Just what is your Miss Pearl teaching you?

Sure enough, there was my letter, marked with a red pen. And next to the part where I said Miss Pearl had called my composition "strong drink," my mother had written, "Is Miss Pearl an alcoholic?"

The bell rang. Holding onto the report card and my mother's letter, I walked in a daze toward Miss Pitt's classroom.

"Oh, there you are, Georgia," said Mrs. Tweed. I looked up, startled. I had not seen her coming. "I have been looking everywhere for you. I have something to show you."

She reached into her purse and pulled out several photographs and held them up. I dimly realized I was supposed to look at them. They were snapshots of floppy-eared cocker spaniels with a younger and much happier-looking Mrs. Tweed kneeling and petting them.

Mrs. Tweed pointed. "That one was named Butter and that one was Cocoa and those were Tea and Coffee." She giggled. "They all had names like that."

"They're cute," I said, trying to sound enthusiastic. "Maybe you could get fish, Mrs. Tweed. I mean, I know they're not the same as dogs, but they'd be better than nothing, and I'm sure Mr. Bottomley would let you have fish."

Mrs. Tweed looked thoughtful.

"Excuse me, Mrs. Tweed, the bell just rang and I have to get going."

Yes, maybe fish would bring happiness to Mrs. Tweed.

17

During afternoon study hall, Mr. Bottomley called me into his office.

"Sit down," he said. "Let's talk about your report card, shall we?"

Mr. Bottomley sat at his desk. He held what I supposed was my report card in one hand and pointed to it with the other. He could have been posing for a portrait. I could draw him like that and put him into my stamp book. Underneath his stamp I would write, "The Headmaster in a kind but firm manner discusses grades with one of his more hopeless students."

"You can level with me, you know, Georgia," he said. "What is it—homesickness? Long way from home?"

I swallowed hard. His words slid into me like splinters. I *was* homesick—but not for La and Winter, and not for the houses they lived in. Those weren't homes. I was homesick for a home I didn't have, maybe a yellow house with a sunny kitchen and a refrigerator full of food. I could feel the tears starting behind my eyes. Oh, Jack, please, please don't let me cry in front of this man who is really a shark.

"Think of ice cream." It was Mrs. Beard. Where had she come from?

"Think of vanilla ice cream and imagine it is right behind your eyeballs and that will keep the tears from coming."

I thought of the vanilla ice cream cones I used to buy from the street vendors in Rio.

I imagined vanilla ice cream sliding down right behind my eyes. And it worked. The tears froze right up. But Mr. Bottomley was leaning forward, offering me a box of tissues. He had already seen my moment of weakness. I pushed the box away.

"Tell you what, Georgia," he said. "I'm going to send you over to our house. Mrs. Bottomley has a nice, homey touch and she'll find something nice to do with you, a little bit of baking or something."

My heart sank. I had not had much contact with Mrs. Bottomley. I had only seen her at some of the evening meals sitting across from Mr. Bottomley, the two of them at the head table like Mr. King and Mrs. Queen.

Mrs. Bottomley was tall and had big bones and big teeth, and I guessed she went to the hairdresser's a lot because her hair always looked curled in exactly the same way. She wore suits, the tailored kind that La wore, and a pearl necklace, and I was not at all sure she was homey or cozy.

Mr. Bottomley rose from his desk and swinging a long arm over, patted me vigorously on the back. "Buck up, now, Georgia girl—we don't want to be disappointing the folks at home."

When I left Mr. Bottomley's office, instead of going to study hall, I went to the art room. I found a pair of scissors and I cut Miss Pearl's grade and the comment "Splendid!" out of my report card. I put them into my blazer pocket to join the pebble and Tim's poem. I cut the rest of the report card into tiny pieces and then walked outside of Dolittle and scattered them to the wind.

The next day I found a flowery piece of notepaper in my mailbox. "Dear Georgia," it said. "Please come for a visit this afternoon at 2:00. I do so look forward to spending some time with you. Cordially, Mrs. B. P.S. Feel free to bring a friend."

I thought about this. I could invite Sid, who would make things easier because she was so loud and outgoing and never had trouble talking to teachers. Mrs. Bottomley might not even notice I was there, which would be perfect. But Sid was so two-faced. We would have a great time, and then she'd come back and make fun of everything to Amy. I could invite Hatty. Hatty would really appreciate it, but it would probably remind her of home and make her homesick. Hatty was too wet to put into anybody's kitchen—she'd leak all over the place. Lulu was the only person I wanted to ask, but apparently it was a crime to associate with anyone who was younger than me.

So that afternoon I headed for the Bottomley house by myself. I was excused from afternoon sports, which at least was a change from the Quivering Fern. I was extremely disgusted with her, anyway. Here I had done everything I could to help her out and then all the Fern could say was that I had a bad attitude.

The Bottomleys lived in a large white house across from Dolittle. I rang the doorbell and Mrs. B. came to the door. She was wearing a plaid skirt, a blue cardigan sweater, a white blouse, a strand of pearls, and an apron.

"There you are, dear, come right in," she said. (Smiling stiffly.) "By yourself, are you?" I nodded. "Well that's fine. We shall just get to know each other that much better, won't we?" (Still smiling, a little less stiffly.)

Her house was a lot like the townhouse in Washington, only larger. There were the same sorts of carpets, the red and blue Oriental kind with the squiggles and the flowers. There were old chairs and lots of books in bookcases, and I felt oddly at home.

"I thought we could bake a cake," she said. "Come on into the kitchen."

She had all sorts of things out on the kitchen table—flour and eggs and sugar and bowls and measuring cups and a cookbook, a terrifying sight to someone who had never done any baking.

"I thought we'd make a chocolate cake," said Mrs. Bottomley. "I didn't know for sure, of course, perhaps I should have asked you, but most girls like chocolate."

"I've—um—never made a cake before," I confessed.

Mrs. Bottomley clasped her hands together. Her face collapsed into an expression of pity, as if I had told her I had lost a leg in the war. "Never made a cake!" she exclaimed. "Oh, my! Well," she said briskly, "it's never too late to learn. First thing you have to do is be able to read a cookbook."

She opened the large book and pushed it in front of me. I stared at the heading "Chocolate Cake" and then at the rest of the words, which seemed to be written in a different language.

Mrs. Bottomley seemed to understand. "Now, Georgia, we are not performing surgery. This really is not difficult." Kindly and patiently, she explained what C. and Tbs. and tsp. meant, and from then on cooking seemed easy and fun. Mrs. Bottomley laughed a lot. She thought I was funny. She laughed at how carefully I measured things and she laughed when I refused to use the electric mixer because I thought that would be cheating.

"Make sure you get all the lumps out," she said, laughing again as I groaned and rested my arm after beating the batter.

When it came time to make the frosting, Mrs. Bottomley could not believe I had never heard of a double boiler, and she exclaimed at the way I hung over the chocolate squares, watching them melt. And when I couldn't believe how soft and like silk the powdered sugar was, Mrs. Bottomley wiped her eyes with her apron and said, "Oh, you are a sketch!" All this laughter. Amazing. I never knew I was so funny.

I liked making her laugh. She lost all her stiffness and seemed kind of girlish. Right at that moment, standing in the Bottomley house with Mrs. B. in her apron and me in another apron, with flour and sweet powdery sugar all over me, and the kitchen warm with chocolate and baking cake smells, it was all very nice. And I wouldn't have minded if it were my house and my kitchen. I wondered what the Bottomley kids were like.

"Where are your children?" I asked, keeping in mind that La always lectured me not to say "kids." (Kids were baby goats.)

Mrs. Bottomley was standing beside me and I felt her stiffen. "We don't have any—children," Mrs. Bottomley said. "Our son died when he was five." Her eyes seemed to get smaller and she didn't blink. "I—I made him a Robin Hood costume and he wore it to bed, and the belt—it had a belt that went with it—rode up around his neck."

Her face was suddenly too close to mine. I could see the eyelashes on the lower lid of her eyes as clearly as if they were the petals of a flower. I suddenly had an overpowering urge to put back my head and laugh and say, "Oh, that's a good one! Ha! Ha! Ha! That's the most ridiculous thing I've ever heard."

Instead, I started to cough. It was the only thing I could do to control this horrible, wild laugh.

"Are you all right, dear?"

"I think," I gasped, "I breathed in some powdered sugar." The laugh was gone now. I had to be careful or I would cry. If I looked at Mrs. Bottomley's eyelashes, the tears would come. "I'm sorry," I was finally able to say. "I'm sorry about your son."

"I don't know why I told you," said Mrs. Bottomley. "It's—you—" She sighed and took off her apron and folded it over the back of a chair. She began to bustle about the kitchen, wiping the table and counters with a sponge. When she turned finally to face me, all the stiffness was back. "Mr. B. and I are so glad we have the school," she said in a Mr. B. tone of voice. Smooth. Grown up. Not girlish anymore. "We have all you wonderful girls to take care of. Now—" She looked at the clock on the kitchen wall. "The cake won't be ready to frost for an hour or so, and you're going to have to get back to the dorm to change for dinner." I knew she was sorry she had told me about her son and wanted to get rid of me. "I'll finish it up for you, Georgia, and bring it over tonight for dessert. Thank you so much for coming."

"Thank you for having me," I said in my best La voice. I took off the apron and put it on top of the other apron on the chair. My hands were sticky, so I didn't shake Mrs. Bottomley's hand, and Mrs. Bottomley didn't move, so I ducked out of the kitchen and found my own way out of the house.

Mrs. Bottomley did not appear at the evening meal. Mr. Bottomley brought the cake over and made a speech about this being Georgia Hughes's first cake. He cut it into a million pieces so everyone could have some and then it was gone. I had been hoping to save it for a while, maybe eating a slice a day, making it last a week or so. The hardest part about boarding school was sharing everything all the time—your first kiss, your grades, your birthday cake.

I couldn't look at Mr. Bottomley without thinking of his little boy in his Robin Hood costume. I wished knowing about this made me like him better, but I couldn't see any hurt in him the way I could in Mrs. B.'s bones and in her big teeth and especially, for some reason, in her eyelashes. But maybe it explained why he was running guns to Cuba, as if he were a grownup Robin Hood, an outlaw or something.

• • •

Dear Jack,
Tonight I added a section to my People Collection, The Women with Secret Tragedies: Mrs. Tweed (I put in a cocker spaniel, too), Mrs. Bottomley, and Mrs. Gross. I don't know what Mrs. Gross's tragedy is, but I'm sure she has one.

Good night, sleep tight,
Georgia

18

At recess the next day there was a letter in my cubby, an airmail letter with a Brazilian stamp, my name and address neatly typed.

Dear Georgia,
I received your report card along with a note from Bill Bottomley, your headmaster, indicating that while you have had a slow start, he is confident you will get yourself on track. Incidentally, Bill was in my class at Princeton. Very active in the Drama Club, as I recall.

I have been busy traveling and giving talks. Last week I was in Brasília and ran into Gilbert Oakes, the father of that pleasant family we met in Búzios at Christmas. Do you remember? He told me that Tim is also at an American boarding school. I am off to a conference with the Argentinians in Buenos Aires next week—much talk about American aid to Latin America, a controversial topic these days. It promises to be quite fascinating. Georgia, I'm sure you can do better at school, just apply yourself. Saudades, minha filha.

Winter (your father)

At the bottom of the letter I saw Alicia Noonan's initials, showing that she had typed it. Maybe Alicia Noonan had also signed Winter's name. Maybe Alicia Noonan had actually written the letter. "Write a letter to Georgia, will you?" Winter must have said. "Sound as much like me as you can and tell her as tactfully as you can not to flunk out of school."

"Jack, I just got a letter from someone who is pretending to be my father," I said.

"Isn't that strange," said Jack.

"I'm going back to being a spy, Jack—full time. This school stuff isn't worth it, and Tweedy-Bird's been acting worse than usual. I swear something's up. I'm checking out the boathouse again as soon as I can."

"I'm glad you're back on the job, Georgia."

"You're a great father, Jack."

"You're a great daughter," said JFK.

19

After study hall that evening, I was in my room when Hatty came in. She sat on the end of my bed. "Georgia, I have to tell you something."

"Hmmm," I said, head in my stamp book. I didn't feel like talking to Hatty. Why did Hatty always want to talk to me when I finally had a moment to myself?

"Just for a sec, Georgia. This won't take long."

Hatty also always knew when she was bugging me, and then she'd say "I'm sorry" all the time until I felt like biting her, but this time there was something different in her tone of voice, less whininess perhaps. I put down the stamp book and looked up. "Okay, Hatty," I said. "What's up?"

"I'm going home," she said. Her eyes, which were usually a wet blue, were clear and shining. Her entire face was shining. The pimples seemed to fade into the shine.

"For Thanksgiving, you mean?" I said, not quite understanding.

"No, for good." She paused a moment to let the news sink in. "I just talked to my parents. They miss me, Georgia. They said if it wasn't working out for me here I should come home. They only wanted me to come because my mum loved it so much, but it's different now, not the way it was when she came here."

I nodded. "I know," I said. I imagined Hatty's mother in old-fashioned bloomers paddling a canoe. But the thought of Hatty going home made my throat ache. She could leave, just like that. The worst part, though, was that I realized I would miss her. She was so much nicer than Sid or Amy. "So when are you going?" I asked.

"Tomorrow," Hatty squealed with happiness. "I'll be home tomorrow, Georgia!"

"You can't wait until Thanksgiving?"

"No, I can't." Hatty sat on my bed and hugged her knees in happiness. She wasn't pathetic anymore. It was as if her bones had suddenly become stronger—her whole body seemed less flimsy. "But I'll miss you, Georgia."

I laughed. "Yeah, you'll miss me for five minutes and then you'll forget my name."

"No, Georgia, honest, you've been real good to me. I wish I could bring you home with me. You'd like where I live, I know it."

I had told Hatty a little bit about Búzios, and it had been a funny thing between us, these two fishing villages at opposite ends of the earth. "It's a good idea," I said. "It's probably exactly the kind of life I was meant for. Are there any yellow houses in your villlage?"

Hatty wrinkled her brow as she tried to think. "Well, there's the McDonald place down by the fish market—"

"I'm just kidding, Hatty, but maybe I could come and visit you some time."

"I'd love that," she said, her eyes shining again. I could see she was already in her village, in her house, in her kitchen, playing with her two brothers, baking a cake with her mother. "Well, I just wanted you to know. I won't bother you anymore. Aren't you glad I won't be around to bother you anymore? I know I have, and I'm sorry." She sprang off my bed. "Well, see you later, I'm going to start packing."

When she left, I lay on my bed and thought about how I had worked at being nice to Hatty lately, but I hadn't been nice enough. She was leaving because no one at Beard had taken the time to really know her. Or maybe that wasn't it at all. Maybe it was that she had a family who loved her and that's where she needed to be.

The next morning before breakfast, the girls in Beard House sat in the living room with Hatty and her suitcases while she waited for the taxi to take her to the airport. Everyone was nicer to her than they had ever been before, but Hatty didn't seem to care about all the attention she was getting. She was already far away from Beard.

I decided that I had been wrong about Hatty. Hatty hadn't been weak, she had just been homesick. She had always known what she wanted, and she had known what she believed in, like the night Sid and Amy had played that stupid game of Truth or Dare and Hatty had stood up for me.

When the taxi came, everyone followed Hatty out into the hall. She turned and hugged me and said, "I'll write to you, Georgia," and her eyes filled up and my eyes filled up and then she was gone.

Abby and Addy were wailing in each other's arms, and Sid's nose was red, and Lulu was saying no one could make her go to school today. Only Amy and Gabriela seemed unmoved. We still had fifteen minutes or so before we had to be at breakfast. I went up to my room and added a new section to the People Collection.

People I admire: Hatty Hickson.

20

In Mr. Tweed's class, I wondered how I was going to get through the rest of the day. His voice droned on and on. And how was I going to stand the Payne, who always had chalk all over her? Now, apparently, she had fallen downstairs or something—those toothpick legs weren't so great after all. She had hurt her shoulder, and her arm was in a sling and the sling had chalk all over it, too. How was I going to face Miss Pitt's hearty laughter over things that weren't funny, and the way she favored certain kids?

I thought about Hatty and how lucky she was to be able to go to school in her own village. All the ages were mixed together, she had said. An old-fashioned one-room schoolhouse. She probably wouldn't get to learn about tectonic plates, poor deprived girl.

In English, Miss Pearl read a poem by Dylan Thomas aloud to the class. The poem was so beautiful it made me feel even worse. It made me want to shed my skin like a snake and start my life all over again. I wanted to go somewhere and write a poem myself—write many poems, hundreds of them, until everything inside of me was on a piece of paper—and then I would throw all the poems in the air and somehow I would be a new person.

When it was time for sports, I knew I would die if I had to go to field hockey. It was time to have asthma. I had learned a whole lot about asthma from La. I probably even knew enough about it to fool Miss Coles, the school nurse, who was a tough old bird. She had been in the army or something, and girls were afraid to go to her because she never believed they were sick and made fun of them. She had given Hatty a hard time because Hatty was always feeling sick, and Miss Coles would smile when she saw Hatty and say, "Dying again, are we, Miss Hickson?"

As I climbed the stairs to the infirmary at the top of Dolittle, I thought of how Amy Glass was always calling me a liar. Well, I was working myself into a pretty good lying frame of mind right now. Miss Coles was sitting in her chair knitting. She stared hard at me with eyes the color of dirty Ace bandages. "Uh, oh, school life getting us down, is it?"

In spite of myself, my eyes filled up. This was dumb. I had meant to describe in very medical terms all the symptoms of asthma, and here I was about to cry instead. I tried to think about vanilla ice cream, but I knew I was not going to get the tears to freeze this time.

"Just tell her the truth, dear. It's surprising how well the simple truth works sometimes."

Yikes. Mrs. Beard certainly had a knack for turning up at the right time, but Mrs. Beard probably didn't know I wasn't used to telling the simple truth. But if she thought I ought to, I would try. So far, her advice had helped me every time.

"My report card," I said. "It's so—terrible. Everything is terrible." I hung my head because I didn't want Miss Coles to see I was about to cry.

"What?" Miss Coles snapped. "What did you say?" Her dirty Ace bandage eyes looked me over. She probably thought I was acting.

"I got a terrible report card, and I—I guess I deserved it." I swallowed. This simple truth-telling wasn't so easy.

I thought Miss Coles was going to faint. She put a hand to her heart. "My goodness—a girl who tells the truth the day after report cards," she said. "That is unheard of." She put down her knitting—pink baby socks, I realized. Wow. Somehow or other there was a little baby in Miss Coles's life. She scribbled something on a piece of paper.

"No sports for you this afternoon," she said briskly. She handed me the note. "Don't make a habit of it," she said, her mouth not showing any bit of a smile.

I wiped my face with the back of my arm and stared at her, hardly able to believe my good luck. Miss Coles took up her knitting. "Go on," she said without looking at me. "I've got work to do."

I ran down the stairs. I found Miss Fern and handed her the excuse from sports. She looked at the note and grunted,

"Well, all right, but we're having a scrimmage today," which was supposed to make me feel as if I were missing something wonderful. Then I realized Miss Coles hadn't told me where I was supposed to go if I wasn't going to sports.

I was free.

Two hours to myself.

What should I do?

I could see the river from where I was standing, free, and sparkling in the sun, just like me right now. This would be a good time to check out the boathouse. What if I really did find guns inside it? I shivered, picturing Tweed and Payne huddled over a bunch of guns.

I started to run down the slope of the lawn, but partway down I stopped and sat and looked all around. Dolittle was perched on top of the hill. It reminded me of "Christina's World." Here I was being Christina, lying in the middle of a field, looking up at a house, that dumb white building where I was a bad, dumb kid. I was glad to be away from it, away from all those classrooms, away from field hockey players calling for the ball, away from the short, annoying jabs of Miss Fern's whistle.

The air was cold, but the sun was shining pretty hard. It felt good against my face. I breathed deeply for a moment, then stood up and walked down toward the river. It was peaceful with the sun on it and the water moving along, and it made me think that my life could move, too. I would not always be the same as I was now.

The old boathouse leaned slightly to one side, and its

yellow paint was faded and peeling. Maybe this was my yellow house. I could live here. I put my hand on the doorknob. Okay, here we go. With only a bit of a push, it opened. I was very surprised—I had expected it to be locked. Now I would have to go in—neck, stop prickling, hands, stop sweating.

Ugh. It wasn't a very pleasant place. Dirty light came in through dirty windows. There was a bitter smell, a dead animal maybe. Boats—rowboats and canoes—kind of like dead animals themselves, were lying there rotting. The old, dead Beard School.

Mrs. Beard, where are you? Why can't you come back and make Beard be the way it used to be?

There was a rustling behind one of the rowboats.

"Mrs. Beard?" Was I finally going to get to see her? My heart raced as a head appeared and then a body. In spite of the gloom, I could see I wasn't looking at a white-haired old lady.

It was a boy. I stared at him and he stared at me.

It was Tim.

Part Three

1

He was big and broad. I couldn't get over the bigness of him, the squareness of his jaw. But his green eyes and the hair falling in his eyes and the freckles were the same.

"Georgia?" he asked. His voice was deeper than it had been. "You look awful. What's that thing you're wearing?"

I looked down at myself. "My uniform."

"That's terrible. You have to wear that all the time?"

"Yes," I said.

"Too bad."

I had dreamed of meeting Tim so many times—just happening upon him unexpectedly, like this—and I had imagined what we would say to each other. I never imagined him saying I looked awful.

"Well, you look old," I said finally.

"I am old," he said. "I have grown old before my time. Like the Count of Monte Cristo, I have been locked away in a dungeon in the prime of my life."

That sounded like the Tim I was used to. But was he real? Maybe one of my daydreams had gotten a little out of hand. I took a step closer and touched his arm.

He felt real. He was solid beneath a dirty green sweatshirt that had a large white A on the front. And he certainly smelled real—unwashed and musty, like the boathouse.

"What are you doing here?" I asked.

"Ran away."

"From home?"

"Home!" he laughed. The laugh was not very pleasant. "Yes, I ran away from Brasília. I took a steamer to San Francisco. From San Francisco I crossed the country by railroad. I was only attacked by Indians once."

I stood very still, hating the prickly way he talked. It reminded me of the sharp edges of his anger that time in the Russian painter's house. But then he stepped toward me and put his hands on my shoulders.

"Georgia. Did you ever get my poem?"

I nodded yes and made myself really look at him. His eyes seemed sort of empty and smaller than I remembered, and less green somehow—muddy, actually, with flecks of brown in them. "I'm glad to see you," he said. His eyes seemed runny now, too, and I couldn't help thinking of Hatty and her endless crying. "I really am," he said. "You don't know how glad. I ran away from St. Andrew's."

"You've been at St. Andrew's all this time? And I've been here and we didn't even know about each other?" I was amazed. I sat down on a rowboat with a thump.

"I knew," said Tim. He sat down next to me.

"You knew? How did you know?"

"My roommate is — ta-da — Ross Callahan."

"Ross Callahan! Sid's brother!"

"Yes, Ross Callahan, Boy Wonder. He told me about his sister — how she was in boarding school across the river and how she was stuck with this snobby roommate from South America."

"I'm a snob?" I asked indignantly. "Is that what she calls me? You should see her — always bragging about her family."

"Ha," said Tim. "Do you think I do not know all about the famous Mr. Callahan, trustee of all the private schools in America? Do you think I don't know all about his planes and yachts and little villas in southern France? Well, anyway, I asked, 'Where in South America?' and Ross said, 'I dunno,' because he is, like most North Americans, ignorant of the fact that South America is not just one big place — that it is, in fact, made up of separate countries. But after a while he did manage to absorb the fact that I am from Brazil, and he said, 'Gee, isn't that a coincidence, Sidney's roommate is from Brazil, too,' and then about a month ago he actually mentioned your name."

"I can't believe it," I said, really mad. "I can't believe you've been over there this whole time. Why didn't you tell me?"

Tim hunched his shoulders. He grabbed a blanket from a pile on the floor beside him and wrapped it around him.

"It's cold in here," he said. I shivered then, too, realizing suddenly that I was cold. He pulled up another blanket for me. "I stole this stuff from the Outing Club. Blankets, sleeping bag, cooking stuff. I'm pretty resourceful for never having been a Boy Scout."

"Why didn't you let me know you were here? It would have made such a difference—I mean, it's been so—boarding school is so—"

"I know," he said. "I didn't call you because if the boys at St. Andrew's knew I had a friend who is a girl, they would have—it's, it's barbaric there. It's full of Ross Callahans. All the boys are exactly alike. You have to play football and laugh a lot with this kind of dumb laugh. Heh, heh, heh." Tim imitated the laugh, and it did seem dumb. "You never just talk to someone. You have to insult them, even people you supposedly like. And if someone is weaker than you, you torment them."

He shielded his eyes for a minute because the setting sun was now shining straight into one of the boathouse windows. Sports was probably almost over, and I knew I ought to be heading back up to the dorm. But how could I leave? Tim shifted so the sun was behind his head.

"Just to give you an idea of what St. Andrew's is like," he went on. "There was this kid, a ninth-grader. Billy. He was small and skinny and looked younger than he was. He had these big, dark eyes, and he looked—newly hatched or something. But he always wanted to fit in with the cool guys. He hung around the Rat Room—that's what they call the place in the basement where we can go smoke and play pool and stuff—it's so full of smoke you can't even see who is standing next to you. Well, Billy would go there, and the guys would just rag on this kid. They called him Betty instead of Billy. They told him to get lost and actually pushed him out of the room, but the dumb kid always came back for more."

The boathouse was growing dark quickly. Everyone was probably back in the dorms now, taking showers, getting ready for supper. I felt little pangs of worry, but I could not make myself get up and leave.

"Billy had a Teddy bear," Tim said. "He actually brought a Teddy bear to school! Ross and this guy Alex put some girl's underpants on it and they held it up for Lost and Found—big joke, get it? Yuck it up, guys, heh, heh, heh. When it was Billy's birthday, Ross and Alex told him they'd put a present under his pillow, so he got all excited and ran into his room and lifted up his pillow and it was a Barbie doll."

Tim's face looked so hollow. His cheekbones stood out in a way they had not before. "Then one day in soccer practice—we do sprints at the beginning of each practice—it was hot, and the coach told us to take off our shirts. Well, Billy didn't want to take off his shirt. I don't know why he didn't, maybe because he was so skinny and he knew the guys would laugh at him—but he really didn't, and he wouldn't. I couldn't believe how this scrawny little kid stood up to the coach. The coach is just an older version of Ross and his friends—I think he's even a graduate of St. Andrew's—right out of the mold—but then Ross said, 'Betty doesn't want to take off her shirt because Betty has boobs.' He got all the kids chanting, 'Betty has boobs, Betty has boobs.' Even the coach was yelling it. Billy started crying on the field. He didn't make a sound, but tears just kept streaming down his face. It was the worst thing I have ever seen. He wouldn't move and he wouldn't stop crying. The coach picked him up and carried him to the infirmary. And the next day he went home. We never saw him again. And Ross just shrugged his shoulders and said, 'If you can't take the heat, get out of the kitchen.'"

"Were they like that to you?" I asked. I curled my hands into fists, wishing I could go and kill all of them.

Tim pulled the blanket around himself and raised his chin a little. "I think they wanted to be, but they were afraid to. They didn't know what to make of me. I'm much smarter than they are. But if they had known about you, believe me, Georgia, I wouldn't be alive today to tell you about them."

Now it was almost suppertime dark, the way it was when we were all sitting in the Dolittle dining room. Oh, yikes! I leaped up and threw the blanket on the floor. What did I think I was doing? "Tim, I have to go."

He grabbed my arm. "You can't go."

"I have to. I'm going to get into so much trouble."

He shrugged. "Just don't go back at all. If you're not there, you can't get into trouble."

"You mean run away?"

"Yes, of course."

"But it's cold here—we can't stay here—where would we go? What would we do?"

Tim glared at me. "I never thought you would act like such a typical girl, Georgia," he said. "Where's your sense of adventure? Don't you see how much fun it would be to figure this out together?" He began pacing the boathouse with the blanket still wrapped around him. "Don't you see how extraordinary it is that you and I were sent to boarding schools across the river from each other and that we had the same horrible brother/sister roommate, and that you are here, now, standing in front of me? It's fate, Georgia. I am the Sand Prince and you are the Sand Princess."

I could barely see his face now in the shadows, but my heart turned over.

"Look, Tim, it's hard to think about right now. I have to go, but I can come back and we can talk about it. I just can't not ever go back there right now."

Tim made a sort of hissing sound. "All right, but you have to come back tonight." I stared at him for a moment. I felt like saying, "I'm not one of your dumb sisters that you can boss around." But then he turned toward me and said, "Please. Please come back. And bring me some food. I'm hungry. And bring your stamp book. Any new stamps?"

Of course I would come back. "It'll have to be late, after everyone's asleep," I said. "But I have to go now, Tim, I really do."

"And don't wear that awful uniform."

"I don't have much else to wear."

I stumbled out of the boathouse and tried to run up the hill, but the cold air and the worry about being late made my legs rubbery. When at last I reached Beard House, the lights were blazing. People were still there. Oh, thank you, I'm not late, I whispered, but the Hag stopped me in the hall. Arms crossed. She was a barricade, and there was no way past her.

"You never checked in after school," she said. Oh, why was it that nothing ever escaped the Hag? She knew how many breaths I breathed today, how many times I peed, how many times—

"Well?"

"I know, I'm sorry."

"You had better hurry and change for dinner." She squinted at me, giving me the Hag once-over. "Where on earth have you been? You're covered with cobwebs."

"Am I?" I mumbled. I looked down at my blazer, which seemed to have white things all over it. Knowing the Hag, she'd guess in a minute where I'd been.

I bolted upstairs to find Sid, as usual, staring at herself in the mirror and Amy slouching all over my bed. It was my bed, my space. Yesterday I would not have said anything to her. Today I had found Tim, and I was a princess.

"Get off my bed," I said.

Amy and Sid instantly exchanged a glance that said, "Who is this peon talking? Did she really say something or are we just imagining it?"

Amy shrugged and stretched slowly like a cat. She got

to her feet and then lounged as close to my bed as she could, her arm hooked around the bedpost. "You never finished telling me why Ross called you," she said to Sid.

"Oh, yeah," said Sid. She peered into the mirror as she tried on a hairband. Then she turned to Amy, eyes wild with delight. "You'll never believe it. His roommate ran away—you know, the finky one he was always telling us about. No one can find him. They've telegrammed his parents and they've called the police. Isn't that incredible?"

The bell rang for dinner. Sid and Amy left the room before I could find out what Amy thought about Ross's finky roommate running away.

2

The maple tree's branches reached right to my bedroom window. What a useful tree! As soon as I was sure Sid was asleep, I opened my window and slipped down. In my book bag was some bread and a baked potato and two pork chops and brownies that I had stolen right from under Mrs. Tweed's nose.

I was glad to be outside prowling at night. It reminded me of my nights on the Rio balcony. The moon was full and beautiful. The river, all black and silver, called to me. I danced a samba down the hill to the boathouse, certain that not a single person was awake to see me.

I was wrong about that. Tim was sitting outside on the dock under the full moon. "You are a wild girl," he said. "What tribe are you from?" He glanced at the sweatshirt and jeans I was wearing and laughed. "Actually, you look completely American."

"I am American," I said and took out the food and placed it in front of him.

"Well, it's better than the uniform," he said. "And this food is great. Is this what they serve you?"

"Yep, it is. What's it like at St. Andrew's?"

"Filthy. Gruel. Bread and water."

"You make it sound like one of those old-fashioned orphanages."

"It is."

"Well, the food at Beard is pretty good, but everything else is terrible. Did you know that Beard is really a cover for a gunrunning operation?"

"What?"

I told him about the Bottomley-Tweed-Payne conspiracy. Tim laughed so loud I thought for sure someone would hear him and come running.

"It's obvious when you think about it," he said. "This old boathouse on the river. And who would ever guess all this was going on at a boarding school for young ladies?"

Just then a boat made its way down the river, its engines humming slightly. "There's one of the boats now," I said. "It was on its way here, but then they saw us and they had to keep going."

"Two schoolchildren unwittingly find themselves in the

middle of a master spy ring," said Tim.

"The jovial headmaster and the scholarly Mr. Tweed are not what they seem," I said. "Will Tim and Georgia be caught in this dangerous web?"

"Not if Georgia runs away with Tim," said Tim. His face was serious now, all the laughter gone.

I shivered. A cold breeze blew off the river. My ears and nose and hands were freezing. I stood up stiffly and crammed my hands into my pockets.

"What's keeping you here?" he asked. "I mean, a school that's running guns to Fidel Castro can't be the greatest place on earth. And Sidney Callahan is your roommate! That in itself would be enough to drive me away."

"Have you met her?" I asked.

"I don't have to," said Tim. "She's a carbon copy of her brother."

"They've telegrammed your parents, Tim, and they've called the police."

Tim scarcely blinked. "Of course they have," he said.

"But, Tim, it's serious—"

"Of course it is, and I'm asking you to be serious, too. This isn't just some lark."

I smiled. *Lark.* Tim was the only person in the world who would use an old-fashioned, bookish word like *lark.* I loved that about him, I really did.

"You need to stay with me," he said.

"I just have to think about it some more, that's all." I was so cold all I wanted to do was get back to my warm bed. "I have to go now, Tim."

"You can't go until you tell me why you can't run away with me." He was standing now, and he had that hunched up look I remembered only too well.

"I can't tell you," I said. "I'm too cold to even think about it."

"I've got blankets and sleeping bags," he said, nodding toward the boathouse. "There's something that's keeping you at this school and you're just not admitting it." He looked at me with narrow eyes. I could see thoughts flickering in his eyes again. "There's something different about you."

I stood silently, trying not to shake. If I stood still long enough I'd freeze into a statue, and then Mr. Bottomley could have me put on a pedestal in front of Dolittle, where you first drive up. There'd be a label on it saying, "Statue of the Worst Student Who Ever Went to Beard." But the good part would be that a statue doesn't have to make difficult decisions.

"Look at the moon," said Tim. "It's the same moon that was shining in Búzios."

"Yes, but this one is freezing."

"Shut up about the cold, will you?"

"I'll come back tomorrow," I said. "I promise."

"You never showed me your stamps."

"I—I forgot them."

"See, you don't care about me anymore." He turned and stalked into the boathouse without saying another word. Arrggh! I stuck my tongue out at him. I knew that I was acting very childish, but so was he.

I made my way back up the hill, alone and sad under the

cold light of the moon. The grass was wet and my sneakers were soaked and my socks were getting wet now, too.

I stood in front of Beard House for a moment before tackling the tree. I thought of the sleeping people inside—funny Lulu and studious Gabriela and cute Abby and Addy and fickle Sid and icy Amy and ridiculous Mrs. Gross and horrible Miss Hagman. It was strange to think of all the time we spent together, as if we were a family, and yet we didn't have anything in common with each other except that we were all at the Beard School.

Climbing up the maple tree was not going to be as easy as climbing down it. I couldn't reach the bottom branch. I stood staring at it hopelessly until I spotted a wooden crate in the grass not far from the tree. It was just the right height, but my hands were numb and I had to blow on them before I could grip the branches.

Halfway up, I panicked. Maybe Sid had shut the bedroom window. Or, even more likely, maybe Sid had noticed I was gone and had looked all over for me and then had gone to the Hag and told her I was missing and the police had been called, my parents telegrammed. But no, the house was too quiet for that—everyone was asleep, and when I got to it, the window was still open. And there Sid was, head on her pillow, snoring away.

I shut the window and crawled into bed. The room was freezing. I buried myself under the covers and tried to make the thought of Tim in the boathouse real. He's here, I thought, my very own Tim, and the same moon is shining down on him that shone down on us that night on the beach. He's here, even if he is moody and bossy and impossible.

3

Tim and I were standing beside the president. JFK was making a speech about how two brave and resourceful young people had saved the lives of innocent Cubans, and the United States would always be grateful that the master spy ring of Bottomley, Tweed, and Payne had finally been caught. There was a lot of clapping and cheering, then JFK turned to me and whispered, *"My own brave daughter,"* and then the Hag was standing over me shouting, "Georgia Hughes."

I sat up in bed and looked around. There was too much daylight in the room.

"Georgia Hughes, get up and get dressed immediately. You'll be lucky if you make it on time to your first class."

I stumbled out of bed, confused and panicky. I hadn't heard any of the bells. Why had Sid let me sleep through everything?

"And what have you been sleeping in? Do you mean to tell me that you go to bed with your clothes on?"

"I didn't mean to," I mumbled. "I was tired—"

"You really don't care, do you, that your father is spending so much money to send you here? You think you have privileges others don't have. I suppose you are just plain used to always getting your own way. Well, I want to tell you, Miss Hughes, that everyone is equal here."

I took a deep breath and stared at the Hag. Rage and fury boiled up inside of me. I thought of the way my father spoke to people who irritated him. "It is not a crime to sleep in my clothes," I said, coldly and distinctly. For once in my life, I felt connected to my father. "Nor is it a crime to oversleep." I slammed my uniform out of the closet.

The Hag eyed me silently. It was the Hag Look, the one that turned girls to stone. I eyed her back. "I can't get dressed if you are standing here," I said. My heart was racing and I was beginning to shake.

"I would like you back here after school at three-thirty on the dot," she said heavily. "It's Friday, and early dismissal, which will give us ample time. There are a great many things we need to go over, your report card being one of them."

The Hag turned on her heel and marched out. I went over to the door and slammed it. The Hag was back in the room in a flash. "Don't you—" and she was the one who was shaking now, red in the face, her sixty-foot-wide bosom heaving—"ever—slam—the—door—in—my—face."

It was all I could do not to slam it again, but I stood frozen for a moment, willing myself not to, and then, when I was sure the Hag had gone downstairs, I threw myself on the bed and buried my face in my pillow. I could not go through another day at Beard, I couldn't.

"Psst—" I looked up. Gertie's face appeared in the door. She tiptoed in and sat down next to me. "You've put Her Majesty into a sweat. She's banging things around down there like nobody's business. What happened?"

I sat up. "I overslept."

Gertie put an arm around me. "Poor thing, you do look pale—circles under your eyes. Why can't they let you sleep in once in a while?"

"I have to get going, Gertie, or they'll chop off my head." Gertie laughed, and I laughed and felt better.

"Off you go, then," she said, giving me a pat as she stood up. "But don't you worry about your bed and things today. It won't hurt you to have someone looking after you for a bit." She gave a nod at JFK. "He looks full of beans today," she said.

"You're right," I said, looking at him. His toothy grin looked even toothier, for some reason, and then I realized with a small pang that I had not thought about him as much lately. I guess I had been trying to do the right thing, work hard and all that. Ha! What had been the point of doing that? No one seemed to care what I did!

"Sorry, Jack, I guess I've been busy."

"I know how it is—I've been awfully busy myself."

That was the best thing about Jack. He never got mad at me the way Tim did, or the Hag, or La or Winter.

I put on my uniform and looked at myself in the mirror

and thought about how Tim had said it was so ugly. He was right — it was, and I was tired of wearing it. Maybe I would give up school and run away with him. Tim and Georgia together — the Sand Prince and the Sand Princess.

"I want to see you at three-thirty and don't be late," the Hag snapped at me as I went out the door.

But I did not speak to the Hag that afternoon. Just as I was coming out of study hall, someone said, "The president's been shot."

4

"What?" I said.

"Kennedy — he was driving in an open car in Texas and someone took a shot at him."

Another girl smiled in disbelief. "Oh, come on, you've got to be kidding."

"No — it really happened."

Suddenly, everywhere I turned, people were saying, "The president's been shot."

Mr. Bottomley's secretary came out into the hall carrying a portable radio. Girls and teachers hunched around it like vultures.

Please, God, don't let it be true.

A man's voice rose over the background of noise. "And now the president of the United States has been taken to . . ."

Oh, God, then it was true. I turned away, not wanting to hear more. I drifted down the hallway, thinking only of how I could get away.

"My dear, are you all right?" Miss Pearl appeared out of nowhere. I shook my head and stumbled quickly past her. I had to get away, even from Miss Pearl.

I stopped at Wilma Beard's portrait in the front entrance. "Mrs. Beard, how could this have happened?"

"It is terrible. The things people do to each other..."

I began to run. I ran out of the building, around to the back of Dolittle, down Christina's hill, down to the boathouse. I pushed open the door. Tim was inside, reading a book.

How strange it was to see him sitting there so peacefully with the afternoon light sliding through the dirty windows. He didn't know what had happened. Maybe I wouldn't tell him. If I didn't tell him, then I could pretend it had never happened.

But there were some things you couldn't pretend.

You couldn't go around your whole life pretending that JFK was your father or that the school you went to was a gunrunning operation or that your mother and father cared one shred about you.

I sat down beside Tim.

"You're back," he said.

"Kennedy has been shot," I said.

"Kennedy?"

"The president. He's been shot." There—I had said it. I wasn't pretending anymore. I would never pretend anything ever again. "He's dying."

Tim couldn't seem to understand what I was saying. "What?"

"The president was driving around in an open car and someone shot him."

"But why?"

"I don't know," I wailed. Then I stopped and tried to get myself under control. "They had the radio on, but I didn't want to hear any more, so I left."

Tim shook his head. "Why would anyone do that?" He was silent for a moment. "I wonder what will happen to my father. Kennedy appointed him."

"I wonder what Jackie and Caroline and John-John will do." My brother and sister. No, not my brother and sister. They weren't ever my brother and sister.

"Johnson will be president."

"Poor Bobby," I said. "And Teddy." My uncles. No, not my uncles. If I had any real uncles, I never knew about them.

"Poor everyone," said Tim. "Oh, watch out," he said suddenly, pointing out the window. "Someone's paddling right toward the dock."

I looked out, and sure enough, a canoe was heading straight for us with two boys in it.

Tim quickly cracked open a window. "So we can hear," he said, "if there's anything to hear. And we can kneel on these cushions and look out and see what's happening, but hold your breath and pray that whoever it is, they don't come in here."

Crouched down on two old boat cushions, I raised my

head just below the window so I could see out. Stalk the Enemy, only who was being stalked?

"It's the football heroes," Tim whispered as the canoe landed at the dock. "That's Ross in the bow, and the other one is Alex Howe. They're the last people on earth I ever wanted to see again."

"Coming to meet Sid and Amy, I bet," I whispered back.

Ross climbed out and tied the canoe to a ring on the corner of the dock. He looked amazingly like Sid. He had the same high forehead, the same blond hair, even though it was mostly shaved in a fuzzy football haircut. I tried to picture Sid with a fuzzy football haircut and started to giggle. Tim reached out and pinched me.

"I can't believe how much Ross looks like Sid," I whispered.

"That unfortunate fact is not cause for laughter," Tim whispered back.

Alex had broad shoulders and was sort of shiny-looking. Amy always called him a "hunk." He had a fuzzy football haircut, too.

Both boys stood on the dock, pacing uneasily. They glanced up the hill nervously, then tossed their heads as if they had hair in their eyes, but of course they didn't. Ross took out a pack of cigarettes and began smoking, and Alex grabbed the cigarette from him every now and then.

"Ha," whispered Tim. "If their coach could see them now."

"Jesus, where are they?" Alex said.

"They're girls," said Ross. "Girls are always late."

And then there they were, Sid and Amy, running onto the dock toward the arms of their lovers like in some TV commercial. Sid launched herself at Ross. She was sobbing.

"What the hell?" asked Ross.

Amy hung back, looking superior. Lucky Sid was now the peon.

"The president's been shot," Sid managed to gasp. "Where have you been? Haven't you heard?"

"Bull," said Alex.

"I'm not lying," said Sid. She tore herself away from Ross and turned on Alex in a fury.

"All right, all right, all right," said Alex, putting out his hands as if warding off a crazy dog. "Give me a break — we came straight from practice. We haven't heard anything. It's kind of a lot to take in." He turned to Amy, the reliable one. "He really was shot?"

"Yes," said Amy flatly.

"Jesus," said Ross. "The president. Is he, is he —?"

"He's going to die," said Amy. "I knew this was going to happen."

"You did?" Ross looked at her in amazement. Both boys were standing still. In that moment they weren't shiny football heroes anymore — they were just kids. Sid was crying, and I felt the tears well up in my own eyes and start to run down my face.

"He was too good to be true," said Amy. "You know how Kennedy was so young and was this big war hero and had this beautiful wife and those two perfect children? Well, guess what? Things like that never last."

Alex shifted his weight from foot to foot. He crammed his hands into his pockets and said, "I don't know. I don't know if that's true."

"It is true," Amy said. She sighed. Suddenly, for the first time since I had known her, I felt sorry for her. She looked so old and sad. I wiped my tears away and I felt old and sad.

Sid threw herself into Ross's arms again. "I just can't believe it," she said, wailing. "It's just so terrible."

Amy sighed again. "I didn't even think you liked him. You were always saying how you hated Georgia's picture of him and you didn't see why you had to have him hanging in your room."

Sid pulled herself away from Ross. She took a step toward Amy. "Just because you never feel anything—just because you're made of stone—you probably don't even care that he was shot."

For half a second, Amy stood completely still. Then she said, "Yeah, right, Sid, just because I don't go around screaming and crying and throwing myself on people just to get their sympathy." Amy turned and walked away.

"Whew," said Ross. He took out another cigarette and lit it.

"I hate her," Sid said. "I really do."

Alex shook his head and took his hands out of his pockets. "We ought to be getting back. It's bad enough with Tim Oakes missing. If they go looking and can't find us either, there's going to be hell to pay."

"Where do you think he is?" asked Sid.

"Dunno," said Ross. "Damned if I care. He hated Saint A's

and Saint A's hated him. He wasn't fun to be around, I can tell you that. I never knew what he was thinking, except that he hated me."

"Come on, man," said Alex. He was untying the canoe. "The place is already swarming with cops looking for Tim. And hey, kid, don't let Amy get you down." He gave Sid a friendly punch. "You're the better-looking one, anyhow."

Sid beamed, and Ross hugged her and said, "Fight the good fight, kid. We'll be eating turkey soon." Sid beamed some more, then stood on the dock waving to them until they were on the far side of the river. Then she turned and went up the hill.

5

"He's right, I do hate him," said Tim.

It was good to stand up and stretch and not be craning my neck to see while worrying about being seen. Tim shut the window, and I shivered. Here it was again, the terrible cold. And fear.

"They said the place is swarming with cops, Tim," I said.

"I heard," he said. "I suppose we'll have to think of where to go." He didn't look at me but began rummaging through his heap of pots and pans. "Time to eat. I've got one can of soup left. Here, open it, will you?" He handed me a can opener. "I want to try to get the camp stove going."

I struggled to get the little camping can opener to grip the can.

"Like this," said Tim, grabbing it from me. "Don't you know how to open a can?"

"I've never opened a can with one of these things."

"Never?

"Don't make me feel bad—it's not my fault—"

I sat and watched him turn the crank. I felt so strange. JFK was dying or dead. I knew I could not make myself go back up that hill and into Beard life again. But could I stay here with Tim and the stupid can opener?

We ate the soup—tomato, or was it to-mah-to?—or maybe there was a third way of saying it that I didn't know about—and some crackers and peanut butter. That was all there was. But the soup was warm, and Tim kept the little stove going for a while so the corner of the boathouse where we were sitting was actually warm too.

Then Tim made a sort of nest between overturned rowboats and canoes. We sat in it on blankets, facing each other, backs resting against the boats.

After a minute, I said, "I'm not learning anything at Beard, no one really likes me, and the teachers don't think I am trying. I'm not going back there."

"I know," he said.

"How do you know?" I asked.

"There's no point to going back. You're not learning anything, no one really likes you, and the teachers don't think you are trying."

When Tim said it, it sounded silly. It wasn't exactly true.

But it didn't matter. I wasn't going back. I would stay with Tim and go and live with him in a sand castle on some beach. For once he looked happy, he really did.

"We'll have fun," he said. "Tomorrow we'll sneak up to your dorm during the day when we know everyone's gone and get provisions."

"Tomorrow is Saturday," I said. "They won't be gone."

"I ought to start putting notches in the side of the wall or something. I'm losing track of the time."

"But maybe tomorrow they won't be around."

"Why not?"

"Because of Kennedy," I said, my throat aching suddenly. How could I have forgotten about Kennedy? For a short moment I had, but now it all came crashing back. "Maybe they'll have a special service or something."

"You don't think of assassinations happening nowadays," said Tim. "It's something that happens in history, like Lincoln. Not now."

"I wish we had a radio so we could know for sure what happened," I said. But what else, in the end, was there to know? John F. Kennedy was dying or already dead. That was all I needed to know.

I wished I had my stamp collection with me, something familiar I could turn to, something I had known before this had happened. I wished I had the notebook with the letters I had written to him.

Who would I write to now?

"Do you have any paper and a pen?" I asked Tim. "I want to write something."

"Of course. Wouldn't go anywhere without it. Have you become a writer?" he asked with interest. He scrabbled around in a backpack and handed me a pad of paper and a pen.

"I do — I do like to write," I said. I felt a buzz of panic. If I didn't go back to school, I'd never write another composition for Miss Pearl again. "I like my English teacher," I said. "She makes us write a lot."

"Good for you," said Tim.

"Good for me?"

"It's good you're writing."

"Oh," I said. I looked at Tim. Mr. Superior. "It's too dark to see," I added, realizing suddenly I could not just turn on a light.

"I have a flashlight," said Tim. "Outing Club special. Come on, get under this canoe so the light doesn't show through the window."

I wiggled under next to Tim. He rested the flashlight on one of the canoe seats. It cast a splotchy light, but enough to see by. He curled up with a book, and I thought for a moment and then I wrote.

Dear Mother,

I am not going to call you La anymore. You are my mother and I ought to call you Mother or Mom or one of those names.

I just want you to know that I think sending my letter back to me was rude, really rude, and if I ever have a son or a daughter who writes to me I will never do that. I only wrote the letter in the first place to make you feel good about sending me to boarding school, but I can see you don't mind sending me away. Did you know you sent me away with only two skirts? At first I didn't understand how you could have done that, because you usually care so much about what I wear. I figured you were having a hard time because of Winter.

By the way, Winter's name is going to be Dad from now on. Do you think other girls go around calling their fathers by their first name? Sid always calls her father Daddy.

Guess what, Mom—Beard is an awful place. The kids are awful, the teachers are awful, the housemothers are gross, and your darling Mr. Bottomley is a phony creep. The only person I like here is Miss Pearl, which you must have realized from my letter, and because I like her, you said mean things about her, like she is an alcoholic. And Gertie the maid. I like her too. And I suppose that's terrible because she is a maid.

But it doesn't matter if Beard is awful because I don't have a choice, do I? I can't be with Dad, and you, Mom, don't want me, so I don't have a choice. I have to be somewhere, don't I? Well, guess what? I have found somewhere. A boathouse.

From your daughter,
Georgia

Dear Dad (alias Winter),
For your info, Bill Bottomley the Third didn't really go to Princeton. He never actually went to college. He is really a spy for the Russians. He is using Beard as a cover to run guns to Cuba. He may even begin running guns to Brazil. I understand the Communists are gaining the upper hand there. They may even be closing the banks down there. Sorry about that, but don't worry — a man like you can always find another job. You will be glad to know I have begun to apply myself. I am getting straight A's now, especially in math. It was amazing how it happened. I said to myself, Georgia, just apply yourself, and the next thing you know, I understood everything. Wow.

I am signing off now. I would have had Mrs. Gross type this for me, but at the moment I am in a boathouse. A boathouse, you say? How strange, you say! Yes, it is strange.

The president was shot a few hours ago. Good thing he wasn't a Republican.

From your daughter,
Georgia M. Hughes

Dear Jack,
I wish you hadn't died. I don't think I can stand not writing to you anymore. I want to go up to my room and get your picture, if I can bear looking at it. I

like this boathouse and I like being with Tim—he is so much better than Sid and Amy—but it is so cold in here.

Your loving—

6

I sat up and rubbed my hands.

"It's cold," I complained.

"Let's get all the blankets and the sleeping bag and get under them," said Tim. "If we go to sleep maybe we won't feel the cold."

We worked together to pile up the blankets and then we burrowed under them. Tim turned out the flashlight. I liked lying next to him. His body was warm and solid and I felt safe. I wondered what the Hag would say if she could see me right now. The thought made me giggle.

"What's so funny?" Tim asked.

"I'm thinking what my housemother would say if she saw us. She would have a heart attack."

"I think a lot of people would have a heart attack," said Tim. "My mother, for one. She sent me to St. Andrew's to get me away from girls. I have always gotten along better with girls than with boys and she hated that. She thought a boys' school would toughen me up. She never seemed to worry about Elizabeth and Ruthie liking boys, though. Everything has always been backward in my family." He was quiet for a moment. "Look," he said. "The moon is up now." He struggled out of the blankets and went over to a window and cleaned it with a sock. Now it made a perfect frame for the moon.

"I'm glad you're here," he said, coming back to our nest. He squeezed my arm as he lay down. I could feel my heart bump. Here I was, a Princess with a Prince.

Clouds bunched up around the moon. One looked as if it had wings. It was pink and blue in the moonlight. Maybe it was an angel. I felt a tiny shiver run up the back of my neck. A long time ago I believed clouds were angels that were looking after me. I think that started when we first moved to Brazil. I had given them names in Portuguese—what were they? Oh, yes, there was Claudia because it was pronounced "cloudia," and Rosa for the pink ones, and Serafina for the beautiful ones because it was such a beautiful-sounding name. I could always find at least one of them in the sky except on rainy days, when I figured they were resting.

Maybe the cloud I was seeing now was Rosa (because it was pink). She had come back because she knew I needed her because I no longer had Jack. And then I thought about Jack again and the terrible thing that had happened to him and I shut my eyes. When I opened them again, Rosa was in wispy shreds, drifting here and there. It was just a regular cirrus cloud. I sighed. When you were little, you could call clouds beautiful names. When you were older, you had to call them what some dumb science teacher told you to call them.

Tim turned over. "What are you sighing about?" he asked.

"Angels," I said.

Tim sat up, pulling the blankets with him. I yanked them back. "Did you ever believe in angels?" I asked. I knew it was something I could ask Tim, just as I knew it was something I could not have asked Sid or even Lulu.

"I guess not," he said after a moment. "But I think I believe in gods and goddesses, like the Greek ones. I think there is a god of the ocean and gods of the trees—of everything, really. To tell you the truth, ever since I've been in this boathouse, I've felt—I don't know—a presence here. It's a weird feeling I get—"

I sat up slightly. "It might be Mrs. Beard," I said.

"Who?"

"Wilma Beard. She was the founder of the school. She talks to me sometimes. Inside my head. I can't really explain it."

"Really?" He looked at me.

"I think so," I said. "Do you think I'm crazy?"

"I don't know," he said. He was quiet for a moment. "Do you talk back to her?"

"Yes, inside my head, not out loud. It's as if I'm thinking-talking to her." As Tim did not say anything, I went on. "One time Sid and Amy were being mean to me, and they locked me in the attic of Beard House. Mrs. Beard gave me the idea of going out the window and climbing down a tree. Sid and Amy still don't know how I got out of there!"

"And you've never seen her?"

I was sitting up completely now. "No, but I know what she looks like. There's a portrait of her at the school. I think she looks like a kid who just grew old in a really nice way."

"Does she talk to anyone else besides you?"

"I think she talks to Miss Pearl, my English teacher."

"Why you, I wonder," said Tim thoughtfully.

"I don't know," I said, and then I yawned. My eyes suddenly felt so heavy I could not keep them open a moment longer. I snuggled down under the blankets. "I'm going to sleep now," I said. "Good night. Thanks for not laughing at me about Mrs. Beard or for thinking I'm crazy."

Tim snuggled next to me. "I didn't say I didn't think you were crazy. But good night, anyhow."

And then, as I shut my eyes, Mrs. Beard said, *"I talk to you, Georgia, because I know you'll listen."*

I opened my eyes and thought-talked back to her. "I try to, Mrs. Beard, but I am worried about something—am I doing the right thing? Should I be running away?"

"That's for you to decide, my dear. I can't possibly give you the answer to that one."

"Tim," I wanted to say, "can you hear her? Mrs. Beard is talking to me." But I was much too tired to say anything, and the next moment I was fast asleep.

7

A little while later I woke up. The floor was hard and I was cold, and the bitter dead-animal smell of the boathouse was in my chest and my throat. I looked over at Tim. He had rolled away from me, taking all the blankets with him. I pulled a blanket off the pile and wrapped it around myself. Then I went to sit on the bottom of a rowboat.

"What are you doing?" Tim asked, sitting up.

"I'm freezing and uncomfortable and I can't sleep."

"I know," he said. "Look at the moon. It's beautiful."

I looked out a window. The moonlight was beautiful, but how much nicer it would have been if Tim and I were in a warm, safe place.

"There's always the attic, you know."

I shivered. Was that Mrs. Beard's voice or my own thoughts?

But the attic! Of course!

"Tim!" I almost yelled. "We can go to the attic in Beard House. The one I told you about, where Sid and Amy locked me in. And if we don't walk around too much, no one'll know we're there."

Tim's hair was matted and there were dark circles under his eyes. "But how can we get in without being seen?" he asked.

"There's the tree. Remember the one I climbed down?"

"But can we open the window from the outside?"

"Yes, I'm sure we can! Come on, let's go! There are beds up there, Tim, and blankets and sleeping bags and a toilet and everything."

"A toilet," said Tim with a grin. "What are we waiting for? Let's go!" He looked around the boathouse. "We can leave this stuff and come back for it the first chance we have."

We stepped out into the moonlight looking like mummies. We wore layers of St. Andrew's sweaters and jackets, and we had blankets wrapped around ourselves in case there weren't enough in the attic. Looking at Tim trying to waddle up the hill, I started to laugh, and then I couldn't stop. I fell on the ground and laughed and laughed.

Tim waddled back to me. "Are you all right?"

Seeing him started me off again.

"Georgia," he said, "have you lost your mind?"

I finally stood up. I was warmer now than I had been all night.

We climbed up the hill and stood at the foot of the tree. "I'll go up first," I said. I handed Tim my blanket and, standing on the wooden crate, pulled myself up onto the first branch.

I climbed up. I passed Mrs. Gross's bedroom window and mine, each on the corner of the dark house. For a moment I thought about tapping on Mrs. Gross's window, but scaring her didn't seem funny anymore. I thought about my empty bed. How strange it was to be out here climbing a tree in the middle of the night. And then my blood froze and I could not climb another inch.

What in the world had I been thinking of? Ordinarily on a Friday I might have slipped away for a while before anyone noticed I was missing. Friday night supper was free seating, and only Lulu might have wondered where I was. Things were a little looser in the dorm on Friday nights, too—we could stay up late and the Hag didn't pay as much attention to us.

But this time, because the Hag had wanted to give me a Hag lecture, I had been told specifically to check in.

Maybe, maybe, in the confusion there must have been over Kennedy, the Hag had forgotten. But then, what about bedtime? Oh, yikes, they'd have the cops out after me, too.

I was shivering so hard I thought I might fall out of the tree. I forced myself to move. Now, more than ever, we had to find a place to hide. I was level with the attic. I could see that the window was open just a crack at the bottom. I guessed I hadn't been able to close it all the way the last time, but my arm wasn't long enough to reach under it. Shivering badly, I climbed down.

"I can't reach the window," I said, my teeth chattering. "You'll have to do it. And Tim, they'll have noticed I'm missing. They'll be looking everywhere for me. They'll think of the attic, I know they will."

Tim grunted and then, without saying a word, he shot up the tree like a Brazilian monkey. In another moment he was back down. "Hand me a blanket and hurry up," he said. "We don't want to let all the cold air in there."

I scrambled up after him, managing somehow to climb

with a blanket twisted around my neck and slung over one of my arms. Tim swung himself through the window and I followed. As soon as we were both in, he shut the window.

"Any light in here?" he whispered. "I forgot to bring a flashlight."

"We can't turn on a light," I whispered back in a panic. "Someone will see it." Tim grunted again but didn't say anything.

As it was, there was enough moonlight to see our way around. There was the bed I had sat on when Amy and Sid locked me in. It looked as if it had been prepared especially for me, with blankets folded neatly at one end and soft squishy pillows at the other. Tim found the other bed.

I lay down and pulled the blankets over me. The room was so wonderfully warm after the boathouse, and it smelled good. It was a long-ago distant-memory smell, a yellow-house smell.

"By the way, you shouldn't worry so much, my dear," said Mrs. Beard. *"They won't think of the attic for quite a while and you will have time to make a decision."*

"Mrs. Beard? Is that you?"

"Of course it is. This is my house, after all. Now, you have some decisions to make, you know, my dear."

"How do you know they won't look for us here?"

"Because you left all that evidence in the boathouse. Very clever of you. They will think you are there and will look all over the river for you. But you must, my dear, do some thinking."

"Georgia?" Tim whispered. "Are you asleep?"

"Tim!" I jumped up, completely forgetting to be quiet, and ran over to his bed. "They won't look for us up here. Because of all that Outing Club junk you left in the boathouse. They'll think we're down there."

Tim sat up. "You're right," he said, a big smile on his face. "You're brilliant."

"I'm not," I said. "Mrs. Beard is. She's the one who told me."

"You're both brilliant," he said. "And this is nice. I'm going to sleep." He pulled the blankets over him.

I tiptoed back to my bed. "Thank you, Mrs. Beard."

"You're welcome. Any time, my dear, any time."

"Can't you tell me what to do?"

"Oh no, no, no. I never do that."

I closed my eyes. I was floating in the warm ocean of Búzios, warm and safe, without any undertow. I could just float and float with my eyes shut for as long as I wanted.

8

When I did wake up, I sat straight up, thinking I had overslept and had missed breakfast again. Then I looked around and remembered where I was and burrowed back down under the covers. I didn't have to get up. There would be no bells, no schedule, no spending the first half of Saturday morning cleaning my room for the Hag's inspection. Saturday was the only day we cleaned our own rooms. We had to polish our school shoes on Saturday morning, too, although I had to admit I actually liked doing that. But no Saturday study hall. Ha. Never again would I have to raise my hand to sharpen my pencil.

Even when thumps and bumps and music started drifting up as the kids downstairs woke up, it was easy for me to ignore it all and just float along. Then I heard a banging not far from my head. I opened my eyes and saw Tim kneeling in front of a trunk.

"What are you doing?" I asked, raising myself up on one elbow.

"Trying to open this trunk," said Tim. "I thought there might be something interesting in it. What I'm really trying to do is not think about being hungry."

I stretched and felt hollow and hungry myself. "I wish you hadn't mentioned it. Well, they're all down there. You can hear them. I don't know when we'll be able to sneak down and get some food."

"Aren't they ever likely to go out?"

"Normally they have study hall. But with Kennedy and everything, I don't know what they'll do. And even when they have study hall, one of the housemothers usually stays around. Tomorrow during church is our best bet."

Tim made a face. "Well, we're bound to face some hardships. There will probably be worse things before we're through. At least we're safe and warm here for now. Maybe we can start thinking about the next step."

The next step. I knew I did not want to think about the next step.

"I can't get this trunk open," said Tim. "I was hoping to find some ancient documents in it, like Mrs. Beard's will. You know, her long-lost will that says after her death Beard should no longer have to be a school and all the girls should be sent home and all the teachers should be fired."

"They'll have to find a job for Miss Pearl, though," I said. "And there's this pathetic person named Mrs. Tweed. She'd be sad if she got fired. And the school nurse, Miss Coles— what would happen to her? And Lulu really ought to be here. She'll get caught up in gangs if she's at home, and no other private school in the world would take a kid like Lulu."

Tim made a face. "I was joking, Georgia. The next thing you're going to say is that you really ought to stay here. Well, I found a book of Robert Frost's poetry up here. It's great stuff. I'm going to write like that someday." He went back to his side of the room and sat on the bed with his book.

I stared at the ceiling. Life was going on downstairs just as it always was, only without me. I could picture Lulu and Sid and Amy, Abby and Addy, and Gabriela, all scurrying around cleaning their rooms. Lulu was probably swearing at the Hag, under her breath, because she hated cleaning her room, and usually the Hag made her redo some of it, anyhow, like her closet, because she always said it wasn't neat enough. Abby and Addy were changing their room around for the hundredth time, and their bureaus and desks and all their junk were out in the hall until they figured out what to do. Gabriela was probably sitting in her room listening to classical music, having cleaned her room the night before. Amy, of course, was sitting on my bed watching Sid clean up, and Sid, in the middle of cleaning up, would suddenly decide to put on new fingernail polish or something. And probably both of them were happy I was gone.

I thought of Sid and Amy and the way they had been down there on the dock—Sid clinging to her brother and Amy so cool. Baby Sid and old woman Amy. Why was she so old? What kind of family did she come from? Could it be that her father really was a Gun Runner? And then I thought of Mrs. Beard. So far, Mrs. Beard had been right about everything.

"Are you going to sleep all day?" asked Tim.

I sat up. "I just had a very crazy thought."

Tim stretched. Sprawled out on the floor by the trunk, he certainly did look funny. His hair was getting wilder by the minute. "What is your crazy thought?" he asked.

"I am going to give Amy Glass my stamp collection."

"That is crazy. I thought your stamp collection was your most prized possession."

"It is. Except for... a few other things." Like my picture of JFK and the moon pebble. But Tim didn't have to know that I had spent hours and hours pretending either that I was his Sand Princess or that Jack Kennedy was my father.

"Why would you give someone you don't like your stamp collection?"

"Mrs. Beard said I should."

"Mrs. Beard?" Tim scowled. "Listen, Georgia, this Mrs. Beard thing—"

"You don't believe me."

"I didn't say that." Tim scowled even more. "I just don't see why you should give your stamp collection to that horrible girl."

"I don't know either, but if I give it to her, then maybe I'll find out why."

Tim stalked away to his side of the room. "Ugh, ugh, and ugh. You don't make any sense at all."

Below us were sounds of voices in the hallway, doors being shut. The house shook slightly, the way it always did when anyone ran down the stairs. The big front door slammed, and we heard voices outside. Tim knelt beside the window and looked out. "They're all getting into a car," he said.

I rushed to look. There they all were, piling into the Beard House station wagon, the Hag at the wheel.

"Good luck," I said. "The Hag is the worst driver in the world. She forgets to stop at red lights."

Tim waved to them. "Goodbye, girls, thank you for leaving. I'm sure I could not have survived another day without eating something."

"What about facing hardships?" I asked.

"Come on," he said, ignoring me. "Show me where the kitchen is." He headed for the stairs and then stopped. "What about the cook? Is there one?"

"No cook," I said. "We eat in the main building except on Sundays. But, oh, yikes, the attic door might be locked."

Tim went quickly down the stairs. The door wasn't locked. I pushed past him and ran down the hallway to my room.

"There it is," I whispered. It looked as if Sid had made only a half-hearted effort to clean up. The Hag must never have come upstairs to inspect. There were clothes all over Sid's bed, and her bureau drawers were open, socks and shirts spilling out of them. On my bed was a sleeping bag.

"Someone's been sleeping in my bed," I said indignantly.

"Someone's been sleeping in my bed, said Baby Bear," Tim said in a squeaky voice. "What are you getting so upset for? You don't want to be here anymore, remember?" He stepped into the room and looked around. "You have so much space and light here. I think my room must have been a closet once or something."

I went to my desk. There was the moon pebble. I put it in my pocket and then grabbed my stamp collection and the notebook with the Jack letters in it. And then I forced myself to look at the picture on the wall.

There he was—John F. Kennedy, president of the United States, my father. He was still smiling, still sitting at his desk in the Oval Office with the American flag behind him. I jumped up onto my bed and began to lift up the picture from the wall.

"Are you crazy? What are you doing?" asked Tim.

"I want the picture," I said. "No one will notice."

"Don't be feeble-minded. They'll notice and they'll know you're near here somewhere."

"Okay," I said. Stupid tears threatened.

"Come on," Tim said. "We have to get down to the kitchen before they come back."

And then I heard music coming from one of the rooms. My heart began to race, and Tim and I stared at each other. Then I realized what it was and I could breathe again. "Lulu must have left her radio on. It happens all the time and it makes the Hag furious," I whispered.

Tim nodded. "Okay. Let's go."

We creaked along the old wooden floor of the hallway, and there at the end of it was Lulu, staring at us as if we were ghosts.

"Oh my Gawd," she squawked, hands to her mouth. She was in pajamas and a bathrobe.

"Lulu!" I gasped. "What are you doing here?"

"What am I doing here? What are *you* doing here? And who is he? Never mind, he's the one who ran away from St. A's. Gawd, Gigi, why didn't you tell me? I didn't even know you had a boyfriend!" Lulu's eyes shone with admiration.

"Is there anyone else here besides you?" Tim asked. He was so nervous he was almost shouting.

Lulu looked over her shoulder and jabbed a thumb in the direction we'd come. "Mrs. Gross stayed back, too—can't you hear that junk she's listening to? Some opera or something. They all went in to town to buy newspapers. They figured they'd be historical, you know, worth something someday."

"They actually said that?"

"Well, Sid did."

"Why didn't you go?"

"I ain't feelin' too good, I guess. And Grossie's here because kids aren't allowed to be here alone. Not that I'd be here alone—the place is crawling with cops. On account of you, Gigi! The whole school's turned upside down because of you. Last night they had us all over to Bottomley's house and they were grilling us about everything. But we didn't know anything."

"There are policemen here?" I almost laughed at the thought of how I had been lying on the bed upstairs imagining everything going on down here as usual.

"Half a dozen, sitting right downstairs," said Lulu cheerfully. "There's one guy who is so cute I die every time I look at him and—"

Tim grabbed my arm and started pulling me back down the hallway.

"Hang on, will you?" said Lulu. "Come into the bathroom. I gotta talk to you guys, and no one'll ever go in there."

"Just for a second," I said to Tim. I didn't want to leave Lulu. Seeing her made me feel more normal, as if the whole running-away thing and the police downstairs were just a joke. I still couldn't believe all this was happening because I had disappeared. Since when did anyone care about the girl who never did her homework?

We went into the bathroom. Lulu sat in the bathtub and Tim and I perched on the edge. I rested the stamp collection and my notebook on my knees. It was the best place in Beard House to hide from the housemothers. Lulu and I came in here at night if we wanted to stay up late talking or if we had homework to do.

Lulu couldn't stop staring at Tim and me. She couldn't stop grinning.

"I just didn't think you were the type, Gigi. When did you get a chance to meet him?"

"It's not like that," I said. "We knew each other before, but we didn't know we were at boarding schools across the river from each other—at least I didn't. Tim did."

"Ha!" said Lulu as if that explained it all. "You've got a lot of nerve. They're looking everywhere for both of you, you know. They figured out you had some connection because of you both coming from South America."

"If you get questioned again, can you lie?" Tim asked. "Or are you going to give it away that you've seen us?"

"I'm the best liar in Brooklyn," said Lulu. "Just ask my mother. So where are you hiding?"

"We were in the boathouse, but it was too cold down there, so last night we came up here." Tim jabbed me with his elbow, but it was such a relief to talk to Lulu, I didn't care what I told her. "To the attic," I said.

"The attic," said Lulu in amazement. "Right over our heads. Hey! That's pretty good!"

"We're going," said Tim.

"Lulu," I said, "do you think you could go down and sneak us some food and bring it up to us?"

"No problem," said Lulu, grinning again. "It's been crazy around here, what with you and Kennedy—the housemothers practically don't notice us at all."

"What about Kennedy?" I asked. Tim was moving toward the door, but I had to ask. "Is he—is he really—"

"Yeah," said Lulu sadly. "Yeah, he is, but you don't know what else happened. They caught the guy who shot him. They showed him on the tube. He must be pretty weird. Who would do something like that? Geez, I'm sorry, Gigi, I know you really liked old JFK."

I stared at the hot and cold water faucets of the bathtub. I knew that if I looked at Lulu, I might break down and wail.

Tim grabbed my arm again and pulled me toward the door. "Check it out for us, Lulu," he said. "Make sure the coast is clear."

Lulu tightened the belt of her bathrobe and pushed up her sleeves. "Ma sent me here to get me away from the gangs, and now look at me. Aidin' and abettin' a pair of criminals. Ha! I'll be back in a jiffy."

But she wasn't, and Tim began to pace around the tub. "That housemother probably nabbed her and made her go back to bed. Let's go."

We met Lulu on the way out. Her eyes were wide. "The cops are coming up," she said breathlessly.

I was so scared I almost dropped my books. And then another thought, treacherous and traitorous, followed. Wouldn't it be best if we just gave it up? But Tim was already dragging me down the hall.

"I'll see you guys later," she whispered, "and I'll bring you something to eat."

Just as we shut the door to the attic, I could hear the

clatter of footsteps in the hall and growly voices mixed with Lulu's sparky chatter. Well, at least *she* was having a good time.

9

Back in the attic I started to pace. What the heck were we going to do?

"Quit it," Tim snapped. "They'll hear you."

I lay back down on my bed and turned toward the wall so I wouldn't have to see him. I wanted to think, but how could I think when I was looking at him? I was trying to think about how I hadn't really known what I was doing when I ran away. I was just running away—from school, from bad grades, from Amy Glass, from Kennedy being shot, from my mother, from my father.

Yup. That was the truth, all right. So now what?

Maybe I was also running *to* something—to Tim. Maybe not to Tim, exactly, but to the Sand Prince. Ugh. Thinking about this stuff was hard.

I rolled over and picked up my stamp collection. Why should I give it to Amy Glass? I'd miss it, wouldn't I?

I could picture my desk in Rio, where I used to sit and talk to the stamps and stick them into my book. My desk was an island in my room—the rest of it was flowery wallpaper and lacy curtains and a bedspread with ruffles and a table with the mirrors where I was supposed to sit and brush my hair and put on makeup. I did not think I was a flowery, lacey, ruffley, sit-and-put-on-makeup kind of person. But what was I? It was only at my desk with my stamp collection that I ever had some sense of being me. Whatever that was.

Starting with Abyssinia, I looked carefully at every stamp I had ever put in. For a long time I looked at the ocelot from Angola. I was tempted to take it right out of the book, but I didn't. I stroked the kangaroo from Australia. I looked at the Belgian lion and the Bulgarian cows, the Canadian Royal Mountie, the French windmill, the pretty Japanese suns, the bright flowers from Liberia, the ships from Paraguay and Peru. I looked for a long time at the largest stamp in the book, the Madonna from Poland. Then I came to the strange, exotic ones from Russia and finally to the presidents of the United States.

There was no stamp of JFK, but now, I supposed, they would be making one soon.

The last time I had put a new stamp in my book had been at the beach in Búzios. All year long I had been collecting people rather than stamps. I turned to the back, where I had drawn Tim's parents and mine and the Russian painter's wife and the headmistresses and Hatty and Mrs. Tweed. And Tim.

I thought that I didn't want to collect stamps anymore. I didn't really want to collect people, either—I just wanted to understand them. I looked over at Tim. Was it possible to understand other people?

Later—how much later, it was hard to tell, though the girls had been back a long time—Lulu appeared. "I never knew there was anything behind this door," she said. She was carrying a grocery bag, which she plopped down on the floor. She began pulling food out. "Popovers," she said. "Soggy, but dee-licious. Sausages. Cold, but I'm sure you will find them oh so nice."

"Thanks," Tim muttered and scooped up a handful of food. "Any news?" he asked her.

"Yeah, you bet," she said. "Your parents are coming here, Timmy."

"Oh, God," he groaned.

"Yeah, and yours, too, Gigi."

Tim went over to his side of the attic.

"He doesn't like me," said Lulu. "And after all I've done for him—risking life and limb to get him some food."

She sat on my bed and looked around. "Hey, this is a real nice place. A sink and a stove and a potty. What else would ya need? A TV, maybe, and definitely a record player. How come Grossie doesn't live up here instead of in that one-room prison cell?"

"I don't know," I said. "Maybe they won't let her. Or maybe she's afraid of Mrs. Beard's ghost."

"Oh, yeah," said Lulu, looking around again, eyes widening. "Does she live up here like you said?"

"Sure, but she's nice, you know."

Lulu laughed. “I sure miss you, Gigi. Sid and Amy are about as much fun as Brooklyn on a Sunday night. Say, you havin’ fun up here?”

“Not really,” I admitted. “I don’t how Anne Frank stood it all that time.”

“Who’s Anne Frank?” asked Lulu. “Does she go to Beard?”

I shook my head. The things Lulu didn’t know were as amazing as things she did know—like how to break into a car and get it started without using a key.

“You know what, Gigi?” Lulu said suddenly. “When it gets dark later, we could give Sid and Amy a wicked scare. Amy’s sleeping in your bed, and we could thump around a whole lot just over their heads.”

“There’s a tree right outside,” I said, the idea making me feel slightly lightheaded. I did have this terrible urge to be silly. “It goes right past the bedroom. We could climb down it and scrape something against the window and call out ‘Sidney’ and ‘Amy’ in a wavery voice.”

“Yeah,” said Lulu. We both started to laugh.

“We’d have to do it before Sid falls asleep. Once she starts to snore, Amy doesn’t hear a thing.”

Tim was next to us in a flash.

“Are you out your minds?” he hissed at us. “They’ll see you. Everyone’ll see you. The police are probably standing right out there at the bottom of the tree! And stop that laughing.”

Lulu rolled her eyes at Tim. I did too, but I knew he was right. I’d climb halfway down and then get so nervous I’d fall right out of the tree and get killed. "We're terribly sorry, Mr. Hughes," Mr. Bottomley would say to Winter, "but she wasn't all that bright anyhow, you know. She really didn't have that much potential."

"It's okay," I said to Tim. "We're just having fun talking about it."

Tim grunted and went back to his bed again. He's impossible, I thought. His word, and it fit him perfectly.

"I'd better be going," said Lulu. "But before I go, I wanted to ask ya something." She hesitated, which wasn't like her.

"Okay, Lulu," I said. "Ask away."

She leaned in toward me and whispered in my ear. "Are you and Tim doin' it?"

"Doing what?" I asked.

"You know—it."

I started to laugh again and then remembered I was supposed to be quiet. "No," I said.

"Kissing, then," she whispered. "Aren't you even doin' that? It must be nice up here in the attic, to kiss just as long and as much as you want."

"No kissing, Lulu," I whispered back, looking nervously over my shoulder at Tim. He was reading. Thank goodness for the book of poems. This was a conversation I did not want him to hear.

"No kissing?"

I sighed. "We're just friends, Lulu."

"How come you're runnin' away together, then? I don't understand you."

I sighed. "It's hard to explain, Lulu."

"Well, I better be goin' now. Nice seein' ya," she called over to Tim. She threw her arms around me and hugged me. "See ya latah, alligatah."

"Wait a minute, Lulu," I said. I picked up the stamp collection and quickly, without thinking too much, turned to the back and ripped out the People Collection pages. Then I shoved the book into Lulu's hands. "Give this to Amy," I said.

Lulu stared at it. "Your stamp collection?" she asked in disbelief. "Why?"

"I just have to, that's all."

"But what am I going to say to her? She'll ask me if I've seen you."

"Think of something, Lulu. You're good at lying."

Lulu grinned. "Yeah, don't you worry, Gigi. I'll think of something."

Just as she started down the stairs, she stopped and came back up again. She went over to the bag she had brought the food in and pulled out a newspaper. "Hey," she said. "I almost forgot about this." She handed me the newspaper, then leaned forward and kissed me on the cheek. "Night, night, Gigi, sleep tight. I'll try to come see ya in the mornin'."

When Lulu left, I felt so lonely I thought I might shrivel up. When they came upstairs to find me I'd be nothing but a pile of dust on the floor. Then I sat on the bed and smoothed out the newspaper. The whole front page had a thick black border around it. Inside the border was a picture of Jackie Kennedy splattered with blood.

It was a shock. And then I was mad that someone had

taken this picture and that the newspaper had put it on the front page. I threw it down. I felt dizzy and hollow and empty. What was I going to do without JFK? I wondered if I could draw him and add him to the People Collection—"Fathers I Have Known."

"Tim?"

"What?"

He sounded grumpy, but I needed someone to talk to.

"Tim, do you know what kind of person you are?"

He came over and he sat on the end of my bed.

"I am the Sand Prince," he said.

"Oh," I said. "I guess I never really know what you mean when you say that. Is that something you can really be? I mean, when you grow up and everything."

"Of course," said Tim. "Naturally my parents think I am going to be an economist or a diplomat." He smiled. "What they fail to understand is that I will live in a castle made of sand on a beach at the edge of the sea."

"Can you really do that?" I asked, in almost a whisper. I knew I shouldn't ask him these things. It was like walking down a road that said No Trespassing. But I couldn't help myself.

"Georgia," he said, and I could see the hurt in his eyes, "it's my way of saying I am going to live as I want to live—I'm a poet, you know."

"But, I mean, can you—" I hesitated. "Can you make a living that way?"

Tim scowled. "You sound like my parents."

"I'm sorry," I said. I knew I sounded terrible, like a grownup, like La, and I felt as if I even looked like La right then, with my mouth all crinkly and small. "I guess I wish I knew so definitely who I am or what I want to be."

"You are the Sand Princess," he said fiercely. He rubbed his face with the back of his hand, and I realized he didn't have as many freckles as he used to.

"I don't feel like a princess. Not even a sand one." I said

"You and I are alike, Georgia—"

"I mean, where are we going to go? And don't tell me we're going to a beach to live in a sand castle, because we're not."

Tim hunched his shoulders and stood up and marched away.

"Okay, sulk," I muttered at him, but I was sorry. I knew I had said a terrible thing.

I went over to the sink and washed my face and hands. We had agreed we could not wash up or flush the toilet because the sound of running water would attract attention, but I was sticky and smelly and grubby. We would have to make a decision soon. I could not stand staying in this attic cooped up with Tim much longer. I was going to go crazy and say even worse things to him. If only I were still in school, I could at least write a composition for Miss Pearl.

Well, it was the weekend. Monday was coming up, and it was hard to imagine not having to do one of Miss Pearl's comps. I hadn't missed one yet. I could be in a bog, in quicksand, getting sucked further and further under, but my free hand would find a pen and write Miss Pearl's composition.

10

I found some paper and a pen and sat down on my bed. Miss Pearl usually assigned the topics, but this time I would have to think of one myself. What should I write about? I tried to think of a Miss Pearl kind of topic. On a piece of paper I wrote

> Imagine you have run away. Describe your feelings.
> Imagine you are the parent of a child who has run away.
> Write about the death of someone you loved.
> Write a story about the perfect place to be.

But which topic should I choose? I looked at the first one. My feelings about running away were so tangled up. Writing might help me sort things out, but I didn't think that would make a very good composition. I looked at the next one. Imagine I am La or Winter ? Oh, no, no, no, no, good grief. Where had I come up with that idea? Until this moment I hadn't thought at all about how my parents might feel about me hiding out in an attic with Tim Oakes.

I felt myself growing very hot and uncomfortable. How dreadfully disappointing, La would say. She'd want to send me to a military school for girls, if there was such a thing. And Winter? Hmmm. He would grin, maybe. "Our little Cinderella is really stepping out," he would say, and he would laugh his awful laugh. I would try to say, "But it's not what you think," but no one would believe me.

But how about the death of someone I loved? My composition could be called "When JFK Was My Father." I would begin, *O JFK, my father with thick hair and a lot of teeth, why were you struck down?*

No, I couldn't write that. The world had just lost a great president, and I couldn't write about his death as if it were my own loss, as if he had really been my father.

So, back to running away. Imagine I have run away. Describe my feelings. What if I wrote it like a story, as if it were happening to someone else? I began to write.

In the middle of the night, Serafina pushed up the window and daringly caught on to the branch of the maple tree outside. The only sound was her roommate's snoring. Serafina's heart raced. Would the housemother wake up?

Oh, ugh. I crumpled up the paper.

What about that last topic? Write a story about the perfect place to be. I began again:

Once upon a time, at the edge of the sea, at the edge of the world, all alone, all alone, ALL ALONE lived the Sand Princess.

I stopped. What was I doing writing Miss Pearl a composition, as if in a few days I'd be back in English class, staring at all the prints of famous paintings that decorated the walls, all the prints Miss Pearl had collected from museums, which covered every square inch of her classroom? My favorite was one of a girl sleeping in an armchair with a kitten in her lap. I always wondered who she was and why she had fallen asleep. And while I wondered that, I'd also be listening to Miss Pearl and taking in her amusement at the things we said or her disapproval, sometimes, or her curiosity about a word or an idea . . . and then I would stare at the paintings some more during the writing part of the class to help me get started.

I picked up my pen. At the top of a new piece of paper I wrote THE SAND PRINCESS.

THE SAND PRINCESS.

Once upon a time, a Sand Princess lived all alone at the edge of the sea in a castle made of sand. And for a long time, although she was alone, the Sand Princess did not feel lonely. She was happy walking on the beach collecting things, shells and bits of driftwood and things, and she'd bring them back and put them in her castle.

Then one morning, as she was on the beach, she saw a boy walking toward her.

"Who are you?" she asked.

"I am the Sand Prince," said the boy. "I live all alone here at the edge of the world in a castle made of sand.

"I am the Sand Princess," said the Sand Princess, "and I live here too."

And then they both laughed, realizing that they had been living on the same beach but at opposite ends and had never known that the other person was there.

"You can play with me!" the Sand Prince shouted in delight. He darted forward and tagged the Sand Princess, crying, "You're it! Catch me if you can!"

Up the beach and down the beach the Sand Prince

and the Princess raced. In and out of the water they played tag all day long. And when they were tired of the game, they played they were pirates with swords of sea-smoothed wood. Next they found smooth flat pebbles and took turns skipping them into the sea.

"Come home with me," said the Sand Prince. "If you live with me, neither of us will ever have to be alone again."

So the Sand Princess took his hand and together they walked into the Sand Prince's castle. As the Sand Princess looked around, she drew in a great breath, for the Sand Prince had also collected beautiful things from the beach and the sea and put them in his castle.

"You may help me collect things," said the Sand Prince. So the Sand Princess walked with the Sand Prince. She walked with her head down, back and forth along the beach, as she looked for beautiful things to bring back to the Prince's castle.

For a long time, the Sand Princess was happy. For a long time she did not realize she was not collecting anything for herself in her own castle.

One day she woke up and knew she must go back to her own castle and see it once more. She walked all the way down the beach, and she thought that the shape of the beach was like a smile, and that made her smile.

But when she came to the end of the beach, her castle was not there. It had been worn away by the wind and the water. Sadly, she began to walk. She had no home now. She walked and walked, over deserts and ice, through forests and jungles. She splashed through lakes and ran down mountains. She was looking for a home.

One day, just as the sun was going down, she found houses, rows upon rows of houses. She stood and looked at them, and one by one lights came on inside the houses, and all the windows turned into warm yellow rectangles and she thought she had never seen anything so pretty.

"I will choose one of these houses," she thought. "One of these houses will be the perfect place to be and I will no longer live all alone at the edge of the sea."

Without even looking it over once for spelling mistakes, I folded the story in half and set it aside. I would get Lulu to put it on Miss Pearl's desk. I felt a tingling at the back of my neck as I thought of Miss Pearl reading it. I thought it was the best thing I had ever written, and it had all come out in a rush. I couldn't wait to hear what Miss Pearl would say about it.

I hoped Lulu would come up soon so I could ask her to deliver the story. I'd also ask her to bring my English grammar book, and I wouldn't mind doing some French, and I wouldn't even mind taking a look at the history book and maybe even the science. It all would give me something to do. Maybe I could even tackle algebra—starting at the beginning of the book and working my way through all the explanations. Ha. The new me.

There were footsteps on the attic stairs. I clutched myself, completely terrified. It was all over — they were coming.

And then I was face to face with Amy Glass.

11

"Amy!" I gasped.

Tim stood up, and fuming. "What is she doing here?" he asked. I could see he was in a rage. I couldn't blame him. This hiding out in the attic business was too nervewracking for words.

"Lulu —" Amy started to say.

"I knew she couldn't keep a secret," Tim huffed.

"It's not really her fault," Amy said calmly. "She told me some bull about how you'd left a note, and she didn't know where it came from, but I could tell she knew where you were, and I made her tell me. I told her I'd tell Mr. Bottomley she knew."

The Ice Queen had been too much for Lulu. I should have known.

Amy looked at Tim. "So he's the guy," she said. She looked back at me. "Not as bad as Ross made out. I don't know what Ross's problem is. No taste, I guess. Just a Callahan trait," she said, and then she grinned. It was the first time I could remember Amy sharing a joke with me and not at me. "I have to hand it to you, Georgia. This is the most exciting thing that's ever happened around here. Your parents are due any second and Mr. Bottomley's having a cow."

Tim groaned. "We have to get out of here, Georgia."

"Let me just talk to her for a second in private, will you?" said Amy, turning to Tim. Even the Sand Prince obeyed the Ice Queen. He scowled, opened his mouth to say something, then clumped over to his side of the room. So much for remembering to keep quiet.

"Listen, Georgia," she said, lowering her voice, "I came up here because—your stamps—I don't know why you did that." She looked at me, squinting.

Amy wasn't exactly easy to talk to. This was the first time since I'd known her that she'd actually lowered herself to have a conversation with me. I didn't know what to say. I knew I couldn't tell her about Wilma Beard. I didn't even really know why I had gone along with Mrs. Beard's idea—just that her advice always seemed to help me, and I thought it would again this time. "I—I just thought you'd like it," I said nervously. "I don't need it anymore."

"You're actually giving it to me?"

I could feel the blood rush to my face. How stupid could I be? What was I thinking of, giving my stamp collection to Amy Glass? "You don't have to keep the stamps," I said. "You probably think they're dumb."

"I act like I think a lot of things are dumb," said Amy. She shrugged slightly. "I don't know why, really." She chewed on her thumbnail and wrinkled her forehead.

"You know," she said, "a stamp collection is something you've had for a long time, something you've had ever since you were a kid. I don't have anything like that. My mom threw everything of mine out. Just like that." She leaned toward me. "Ever known someone who drinks—I mean, really drinks? Like has fits and falls down and passes out?"

It was hard to look at Amy. Her face was so tight, and I had never heard anyone talk the way she was talking—I mean so totally honestly. She made me feel young and scared, as if I didn't know anything about anything.

"My mother would drink and then say there was too much clutter around the house, and the next thing you knew, everything I cared about was gone."

"I'm sorry," I managed to say. Something fell to the floor over on Tim's side. What in the world was he doing? I kept hearing him walking around.

"I know that stamp collection means a lot to you," Amy said, lowering her voice. I could see she didn't want Tim to overhear our conversation. "I can't believe you gave it to me. I haven't exactly been nice to you." I bit my lip. Mrs. Beard had been so right. How had she known? How did she always know so much? "I can't actually remember the last time anyone gave me anything," Amy said thoughtfully. "So when you gave me your stamps, I was really—"

"I'm sorry I took your room and your roommate," I blurted out.

"Is that why you gave it to me? Look, that wasn't your fault," she said. "But it was an easy thing to be mad at you about. I think I was really mad at you because you're always just yourself. You don't seem to need to be cool or popular."

I shook my head. That was the craziest thing I had heard in a long time. Me, always being myself. I didn't even know who myself was. Only a short time ago I had thought I was a Sand Princess! What would Amy think about that? What would Amy think about Tim if she really knew him? He was kneeling in front of the window and staring. I was glad Amy was speaking softly. I hoped Tim couldn't hear her. I had a feeling he might make fun of her. He always seemed to find the weak spots in people.

"I'm not allowed to live with my mother anymore," Amy went on, speaking softly and very slowly. Her voice shook a little. I wondered suddenly how many people she had talked to about this. Maybe not even Sid? But why me? Because I had given her my stamp collection?

"My father got fed up a long time ago. He moved out and took me with him, and then he met someone else and they had kids, and I just didn't feel like they wanted me around. So I guess that's why I'm here," she said. "The weird thing is—it's better being here than at home. Don't you think that's weird?"

"No," I said. "I can understand that. I—I—" I took a deep breath and then, very quietly, so Tim couldn't hear, I said, "My father—he met someone else, too."

"Wow," said Amy. A look of understanding crossed her face. "I get it now. That's why you said he died. Yeah, it feels like that when it first happens. It feels like they've died and just left you."

My heart leaped out to Amy. I couldn't believe I had told her what I hadn't told anyone else. And I couldn't believe how light it made me feel, as if some horrible trash inside of me had been cleaned up. Had Mrs. Beard known that Amy and I would end up talking like this? That she and I were the only people we could tell our terrible secrets to?

"Georgia," said Amy. "I'm sorry we locked you in the attic that time."

"It's okay," I said. "It wasn't so bad."

"How did you get out that day?" she asked.

I sighed. "Mrs. Beard—" I started to say, but Amy's old snotty expression came back, and she stood up.

"Never mind," she said. "You don't have to tell me." She was quiet for a moment. I could see that being nice wasn't natural for her, that maybe she had used up her niceness for the day. "You wouldn't believe how upset people are that you're gone, Georgia. Mrs. Tweed and Mrs. Bottomley and Miss Pearl—you'd think you were their own kid or something. And Miss Coles! You'd think there was a war on—she's trying to mobilize the troops. And then there's Gertie! Gertie, the maid, if you can believe it, comes in and refuses to go until you've been found!"

Oh, Gertie! I hadn't thought of her at all when I ran away.

Tim was banging around again. I wished he would stop. As it was, I couldn't believe they hadn't thought of looking for us here. Maybe Mrs. Beard was helping us somehow in that way, too. Distracting the cops with false clues. I smiled at the thought.

"I have to go," said Amy. "But what are you going to do? You can't stay here."

I shook my head. "I don't know," I said.

Amy looked at me long and hard. "Well, see ya, Georgia, good luck."

And she left.

12

"What did she want?" asked Tim, coming over. "I thought she'd never leave. Listen, Georgia, there's a barn not far from here. I passed it on my way here."

I looked at him blankly. "A barn?"

"As soon as it gets dark, we can slip out."

"And then what?" I asked.

"I'll figure it out," he said. "I've almost got my stuff together."

"Oh," I said, not even really listening to him. He went back to his side of the room. I picked up the People Collection. There was still room on the last page for a few more people. I found my pen and wrote, "People Who Care about Me."

I drew a picture of Amy Glass. I drew one of Lulu LaBombard and Hattie Hickson. And one of Miss Pearl. And Mrs. Tweed. (No cocker spaniel this time.) And Mrs.

Bottomley. And Miss Coles. And one of Gertie, with her big eyes and her big smile.

I thought about my parents coming to Beard — La leaving the townhouse in Washington, Winter flying up from Brazil. Fifteen hours on an airplane. He must have left the moment he received the telegram. Or was he sending his secretary in his place? Did my parents really care about me, or were they just coming here because they had to? I would have to wait and see.

Wait and see? I would be hiding out in a barn with Tim Oakes. I wouldn't see anything.

I put the pages of the People Collection down on the floor and lay back and closed my eyes. I wished I could just sleep and sleep and sleep so I wouldn't have to think anymore. And when I woke up I'd be far away in my yellow house with the refrigerator stuffed with food. But the oddest thing was, when I pictured the yellow house, it was full of all those people I'd just finished drawing — Amy and Lulu and Gertie and all of them. And strangely, the house wasn't yellow at all anymore, but white. It was an old white house with an attic, and in the attic was an old lady who talked to me.

"Georgia!" I looked up, startled. Tim was standing in front of me. "It's time to go, Georgia."

I realized the room had grown dark.

"You hand me the stuff and I'll go down the tree."

I sat on the bed and didn't say anything.

"Come on," he said.

"I'm not coming," I said.

"Of course you're coming," he said.

"I can't," I said.

Tim exploded into a series of laughs, almost like sneezes. "What are you going to do?" he asked.

I couldn't look at him. "I'm staying here," I said.

"Here?" He sort of grunted at me. "But you can't," he said. "That's the whole point. They're going to find us in probably less than two minutes because those two girls down there are going to spill the beans just as soon as our parents arrive and get their claws into them."

"I mean, I'm staying here at this school."

Tim put back his head and laughed. I thought of all the times I had been proud of being able to make him laugh. Well, I wasn't proud now.

"You're going to stay here, at the weird Beard School?" he said. "That's a good one. And why is that, may I ask?"

My face was burning. "I'm at home here," I said. "At least more at home here than any other place I've been, and that's saying a lot."

"That's not saying a thing."

I picked up the People Collection. I knew what I had just drawn there was true. "The people here care about me. And," my voice stuck a little and I had to clear my throat, "I care about them."

"You want to stay in a mediocre boarding school with lunatics for housemothers and stuck-up kids for roommates," said Tim. His eyes were red. He looked as if he hadn't really slept in weeks. Well, he probably hadn't.

"It's what I want to do right now," I said. I stood up. I didn't know how much strength I had to fight Tim. I wished he would just leave. "It's not like I'm going to be here for the rest of my life."

Tim took a step toward me, and then he grew very still, the way he had on the beach at Búzios just before he kissed me. "All right, Georgia," he said. "If that's what you want to do." He walked away. No more kisses from Tim, not ever again. "I'm going now," he said.

He had all his things stacked neatly in a pile by the window—his sleeping bag and the book of poems (he was stealing it), and a St. Andrew's sweatshirt. He stashed the book in his pocket and then tossed everything else out the window. He swung himself out to the tree. "Wait," I said. I fished the pebble he'd given me out of my pocket. "I want you to have this. It's like the moon."

He reached out to take it and then he actually smiled. "Goodbye, Sand Princess," he said. "Maybe we'll meet again on some beach at the edge of the sea."

And then he was gone.

I sat down on my bed. I found the picture of him I had drawn less than a year ago. With a shaking hand, I wrote underneath it, "People I Have Loved."

Then I walked down the attic stairs, pushed open the door, and forced my trembling legs to march into the River Room. Sid was at her bureau, gazing deeply into the mirror as she put on lipstick. Lulu and Amy were sitting on my bed. I leaned against the doorway.

"Get off my bed," I said, and Lulu started screaming,

"Oh my Gawd, she's back, I can't believe it!" And while I was thinking about how the next thing I was going to have to do was face my mother and father, Lulu and Sid and Amy were all hugging me.

"Oh, my dear," said Wilma Beard. *"Welcome home."*